MW00936214

FINDING LOVE AT STEEPLE RIDGE

A BUTTARS BROTHERS NOVEL, STEEPLE RIDGE
ROMANCE BOOK 2

LIZ ISAACSON

AEJ CREATIVE WORKS

ISBN-13: 978-1978188860

ISBN-10: 1978188862

"And I will bring the blind by a way that they knew not; I will lead them in paths that they have not known: I will make darkness light before them, and crooked things straight."

— ISAIAH 42:16

1

Ben Buttars thundered down the stairs, a bit of dust rising into the air from his boots. Or maybe that was from the wooden stairs that hadn't been swept in a while. The boss hired a maid service that came in twice a month, but once spring thawed and all the mud dried to dirt, not even a daily cleaning could keep the two-story house dust-free.

"Something smells good," his oldest brother, Sam, said as he pushed through the back door and into the kitchen, where Ben had just entered. He snatched a pair of oven mitts from the counter and opened the door to a blast of heat.

Ben flinched away lest he get burned. "Soft pretzels. Your afternoon snack." He grinned, though the memory of his mother always came with the sight and smell of the last snack she'd made for him before she died. Ben had perfected her recipe over the past ten years.

"Mustard?" Sam bent to look in the fridge.

"Already on the counter. Ketchup too." Ben slid the sheet tray onto the stovetop and gazed down at the perfectly browned snack.

"No one eats ketchup on pretzels," Sam said.

"I do." Ben tossed him a grin just as both of their phones sounded. He groaned while Sam simply checked his without any alarm on his face. But Ben was supposed to have the afternoon off before meeting with the recreational director about...something his boss had seemed deliberately dodgy about. And he'd been planning to stuff himself silly with salty pretzels and ketchup.

"Horses out above pasture six," Sam said, lifting his eyes to Ben's. Out of his three brothers, Ben looked the most like Sam—the most like their father, who'd had eyes the color of russet potato skins and hair several shades darker than that. The twins, who sat in between Ben and Sam, had lighter hair and their mother's darker eyes. All four boys had freckles and broad shoulders and a love for the outdoors.

Only Ben had been a minor when their parents had passed away. Only Ben had been forced to leave high school before he'd graduated. Only Ben hadn't dated someone in the last decade.

"Right now?" he asked, and he hated that it sounded more like a whine than a question.

"Right now." Sam started toward the back door, smashing his cowboy hat lower onto his head.

"But the pretzels—"

"They'll keep." Sam's voice filtered back toward him just before the screen door slammed. Frustration threaded through Ben. "They'll keep" was Sam's standard answer for everything.

What should we do with Mom and Dad's stuff?

It'll keep.

Shouldn't we go back to Wyoming? Sell the house?

It'll keep.

Ben cast one last look at the steaming pretzels—which would be ten times better hot—before following his brother out of the house they shared. The blue May sky of Vermont stretched before him, the barns and public parking areas of Steeple Ridge Farm just steps from the house.

The pastures, however, lay to the north and west, in the same direction of the wooded area where Ben liked to let his horse wander after a long day of farm work. He strode toward the back barn, where they housed the farm's horses, including his mare, Willow.

Her dark brown coat glistened, because Ben took immaculate care of her. He'd allow dust in the house, but certainly not on his horse. "All right, girl," he said as he put the saddle on and cinched it. "Let's do this quickly, okay? Because I made pretzels." He led the horse out of the barn and swung onto her back.

Steeple Ridge boarded horses, and the five they had from a barn in northern New York had been nothing but trouble since they'd arrived last week. They seemed to have a knack for finding —or creating—weaknesses in fences and running wild through the woods until they came to the stream.

Bracken ferns grew there, and these New York horses seemed to have developed a taste for it, though if they ate enough of it they could experience a loss of nerve function. As the manager of the boarding stable, Sam didn't much want to return nerve-damaged horses to the New York clients. With hot pretzels still on his mind, saving the horses from their own fern obsession was a toss-up for Ben.

He joined his brothers and they spread out into the woods, ropes at the ready. The owners of the farm, Tucker and Missy Jenkins, had gone into town to purchase supplies for the upcoming weekend barbeque, or they'd be saddled up and rope-ready too.

Ben whistled as he ducked under a tree branch. A rustling sound to his left drew his attention, and he had one of the New York devil-horses roped a few seconds later. One of them, though, eluded all the brothers until finally Ben couldn't take it anymore.

"How about I take these four back?" he asked Sam, trying to make it sound like he didn't care if he went or not. But he feared that if he didn't go in the next five minutes, he wouldn't even have time to scarf down a single bite of pretzel before his meeting with the recreational director.

He searched his memory for her name but came up blank. While he and his brothers had arrived at Steeple Ridge at the end of last summer, he didn't get into town for much more than church. And even then, he didn't always attend.

There was something soothing and peaceful about the woods, and sometimes the Sabbath simply found him communing with nature, which allowed him to feel closer to God. It had taken him a good five years to accept that God was still loving, still wise and omnipotent, after his parents' plane crash. Sometimes being outside with only trees, birds, and sky reminded him of God's power better than anything a pastor could say.

"Go on, then," Sam said. "Darren, you stay with me. Logan, help 'im get those horses properly secured. Lots of water."

In another situation, Ben might have asked if his brother thought any of the horses had already consumed something poisonous out in the woods, but today, he didn't. He simply set Willow toward the farm and urged her to go a little faster than he would have normally.

"Is there a fire?" Logan asked, coming up beside him.

"I made pretzels," Ben said.

Logan laughed, a big, boisterous sound that filled the sky with noise—and Ben's blood with annoyance. "You and your pretzels."

"I don't see you complaining when you eat them." Ben nudged Willow again and she almost picked up her trot.

"Nope," Logan said. "Never will. I don't know how you get them so stretchy and crispy at the same time. It's amazing."

Some of the tension drained from Ben's shoulders, and he grinned at his next oldest brother.

"Ah, spicy brown mustard," Logan said. "We have some, right?"

"Dunno." Sam did all the grocery shopping for the brothers. "If you put it on the list at some point, I'm sure we do."

They arrived back on the farm and got the horses brushed down and properly secured in their box stalls. By the time Ben had Willow safe and secure, the very idea of a pretzel had faded to a dot on the horizon. Because he was now late for his appointment.

Sure enough, when he exited the barn, a shiny black sedan sat in the public parking lot. The car looked like it had never been on a farm.

"There you are."

He turned at the feminine voice to find a tall, athletic brunette striding away from the house and toward him. She'd definitely never been on a farm either. Ben drank in the length of her legs, very aware of the pinch of interest in his chest. Her dark brown ponytail swung from side to side, and Ben wondered what her hair would feel like between his fingers.

He swallowed. This woman was so far out of his league, he couldn't even get there in a rocket ship. She paused a healthy distance from him, cocked her hip, and folded her arms. "Which one of you is Ben?"

He glanced at Logan, who wore an expression of half-horror, half-surprise. "He is." Logan hooked his thumb at Ben and walked toward the house. Once he'd passed the beautiful woman, he turned back and beamed for all he was worth, lifting both arms in victory. "I'll save you a pretzel!" he called before turning around and hurrying into the house.

Ben waved at him like it was no big deal, that pretzels didn't matter at all That river of desire built into something bigger even as he tried to tame it. "I've forgotten your name," he said. "Missy told me, but." He laughed, the sound so full of nerves he wondered how his brothers had ever figured out how to talk to a woman, hold hands with a woman, kiss a woman. Not that they dated all that much, but Sam had had a girlfriend or two, and Logan was definitely a charmer. He could talk to women all day, and Ben had watched him do it, trying to discover the secret. So far, he hadn't figured much out.

His stomach twisted and his mouth went dry dry dry. He'd just forgotten his own name, let alone hers.

"Reagan Cantwell," she said, coming forward again. She extended her hand toward him to shake. He did, trying not to notice the softness of her skin or the strength in her touch. Or the beauty in the lines of her face. Or the depth of her eyes.

She existed on another planet, where men with a lot of money existed. More talent. More brain cells.

"My friends call me Rae."

"Like a ray of sunshine." He smiled but when she didn't, he wiped it from his face quickly, pure foolishness flooding him.

"So Missy tells me you'll have all the info on the horseback riding lessons she wants the rec center to sponsor."

When he stood there, his thoughts stampeding like those crazy New York horses, she lifted her eyebrows as if to say *Well?*

Ben stumbled back a couple of steps. "The horseback riding lessons. Right. Yes. I know about that." And though he didn't really know what a partnership would look like, he walked forward, drew in a deep breath of her scent and got a noseful of angel food cake and chocolate.

His mouth watered but he still managed to say, "I have all the details in the office in the house. You want to come in?" He'd never been more relieved than when she came with him. And the folder Missy had put on the desk in the office really calmed him. So he hadn't looked at it yet. He could wing this meeting—as long as he didn't look directly at Rae. If he did, he might not even remember how to ride.

2

Reagan Cantwell couldn't believe she'd let Missy persuade her out to Steeple Ridge, even if they'd been friends for two decades. She didn't fit here; she never had. And she was needed badly at the Sports Complex, where a teen softball tournament was set to start the following day. It was Rae's job to ensure the fifty-five acre outdoor facility was ready for the swarms of people about to descend upon it. That meant no trash on any of the twenty-eight soccer fields, lots of extra paper towels and supplies for the restrooms, stocking and staffing the concession stands, and ensuring the five baseball fields were raked and ready.

She sighed as Ben opened the screen door and stood back, waiting for her to enter. The scent of baking bread and salt met her nose, reminding her that she hadn't eaten lunch yet though it was nearly time for dinner.

Rae managed the entire complex and the twenty-two-man crew it took to maintain it. She rarely sat down to eat, though she did have an office at the recreation center in town. Now that May had arrived, Rae's job was in full swing and would be until the end of August.

"Something smells good," she said, giving the cute cowboy the smile he'd sought earlier.

His grin returned, this time brighter than before. She liked it. Liked his straight teeth. Liked the gentle air surrounding him. Liked his tanned skin and wide shoulders and sexy, black cowboy hat.

Stop it, she told herself as she entered a kitchen where the other cowboy had already helped himself to one of the pretzels. *You're not dating a cowboy. Not again. You're not dating anyone for a while, remember?*

The other cowboy dunked a chunk of pretzel into dark brown mustard and took a bite. Rae's mouth watered and Ben squeezed past her. "You want one?"

"Oh, no." She half-laughed as she waved her hand. She swallowed her saliva but couldn't tear her eyes from the baked goods on the stovetop.

"Mustard or ketchup?" Ben asked as if she hadn't declined.

"Who eats ketchup on a pretzel?" she asked.

Ben frowned and muttered something under his breath as he used a pair of tongs to lift two pretzels onto a paper plate. He spooned a bit of mustard onto the plate and grabbed the whole ketchup bottle. "Office down the hall." He nodded for her to go first, and she moved further into the house.

A bathroom sat on her right, with the office straight ahead. Another door waited to the left, but it was closed. She entered the office and took a seat in front of the desk while Ben set down the food and walked around to the other side.

"I like ketchup on pretzels," he said. He squirted way too much of the condiment onto another plate and snagged his pretzel from hers.

"Who made these?" Rae asked as she tore off a piece.

"I did."

Surprise flitted through her and her taste buds exploded with her first bite. A quiet moan emanated from her mouth and she relaxed for probably the first time that month.

"I didn't know cowboys could bake," she said once she'd eaten almost half of her pretzel.

"Some of us had to learn a lot of things early."

Something lingered there, just below the surface of his skin, just behind that pair of gorgeous eyes. Something Rae very much wanted to find out.

She wondered why she'd ever thought she should pawn this ridiculous idea of community horseback riding lessons—and Ben—onto someone else at the rec center. She hoped that maybe starting another relationship wouldn't shred her heart too badly. She prayed that Ben was older than twenty-one. He didn't look much older than a high school graduate....

Please, Lord, she thought. *Anything over twenty-one is acceptable, okay?*

Ben spoke in his deep, bass voice, which sent rumbles down her spine. She managed to listen as he showed her some mock registration forms and outlined how Missy wanted more kids out on the farm so they could get more youth into equestrian care than were currently interested.

"Who will do the lessons?" she asked.

"Missy will handle the beginners." He sighed, and she found frustration in his face. "I'll probably be assigned the others."

"You don't seem happy about that."

Ben ran his hand over his clean-shaven jaw and looked away. "I'm not particularly adept at horseback riding lessons."

"You can ride a horse, yes?" She cocked her head and played with the end of her ponytail. Classic flirting gestures, but Ben didn't seem to notice at all.

"Yeah, sure." He gathered all the papers and set them back in the folder before closing it. "I don't really like teenagers either." He cleared his throat and swiped his finger through a spot of ketchup on his plate.

"How much older—I mean, you're not a teenager, right?"

Ben's eyes, which had been flitting all over the place, zipped to hers. "What?"

Rae forced a laugh out of her chest and up her throat. "I mean, of course you're not a teenager." She leaned forward. "How old are you?"

Ben blinked. His mouth worked and he managed to say, "Uh...."

The fight left Rae's body. "Just nod if you're older than twenty-one."

He nodded once, twice, three times, almost like his neck couldn't do much more than that.

Relief washed through her veins, and she slumped back into her chair. "All right then." She reached for the folder, the weight of her schedule suddenly pressing on her shoulders. "I'll take this and go over it with my boss and let you know."

She stood and left the office, left the charming farmhouse with its delicious scent of cowboy and freshly baked pretzels. She made it to her car, feeling slightly less crazed than she had inside.

"Not dating," she muttered to herself as she slid into the car and put Steeple Ridge in her rearview mirror. With every passing yard, her erratic feelings over the cowboy settled and that sense of dread that had been plaguing her since Missy had called and set up the appointment returned. Honestly, it was better than that fiery attraction between her and a cowboy that had to be just barely older than twenty-one.

————

"CALL ZACKARY MCCOY," SHE INSTRUCTED HER CAR AS SHE maneuvered back into the populated part of Island Park. The Sports Complex sat on the northern side, just across the street from the elementary school, and she set her car in that direction.

"What's up, Rae?" Zack answered, then immediately continued a conversation with someone with him wherever he was. Probably in his office, which sat right across the hall from hers.

Rae waited for him to finish, then said, "Who else can take on these horseback riding lessons?" As much as she wanted to be in Ben's presence and learn about what he hid behind those shuttered eyes, she thought their working together wouldn't be a smart idea. And now that she was thirty-five, she needed to be smart about a lot of things she hadn't considered in the past.

Zack exhaled, the sound one long hiss over the phone line. "I can check our staff, but we're already in the weeds with lifeguards, pool concessions, the senior citizen class, the—"

"All right." Rae's words had more bite than she liked, but she couldn't help it. Heading into summer was the worst time for the community rec center in terms of staffing, and Rae knew it. She'd been the human resources administrator for three years before moving over to manage the youth sports programs, and eventually, the Sports Complex.

"Let's see where we are in the next three weeks," Zack said in his placating tone. Out of all the men she'd dated in Island Park, her relationship with him had been the best. Absolutely no spark between them, which allowed them to remain friends all these years later. But she still missed the camaraderie, the feeling of belonging to someone, the assumption that she wouldn't have to eat alone that night. Or worse, with her equally single mother. Sure, she loved her mother. Liked spending Sunday afternoons with her. But Friday night? Rae didn't quite want *that* relationship with her mom.

"I'm at the Sports Complex," Rae said, though she was still several blocks away and ended the call. She really didn't have time to create, conceptualize, and carry out the horseback riding lessons. She wouldn't have time even if she somehow figured out how to clone herself. Even though she'd been a champion show rider once, she hadn't been on a horse in years and years. Had no desire to saddle up again.

No desire to give her heart to another cowboy only to have it handed back in tatters.

She pulled into the parking lot and came to a stop in the circle drive closest to the restrooms and the children's playground. She should've gone around through the neighborhood to the east, parked over by the supply shed on the edge of the complex. But she needed the walk, the fresh air, and with any luck, she'd be able to sort through her tangled emotions before she had to meet with her guys.

The sunshine warmed her skin where the air conditioning had cooled it. The spring smell of pollen lingered in the air, and the evidence that her crew had been working most of the day showed in the pristine, green lawns, free from trash and weeds. A breeze played with her ponytail and she took several deep breaths, her thoughts calming with every step she took around the mile and a quarter loop.

Her gaze wandered to a lower spot of grass that had once been a pond. The town filled it in the summer before she'd taken over the complex after a four-year-old boy had drowned in the murky water. His mother still lived in town, and Rae was glad the constant reminder didn't exist anymore. She almost made a mental note to go visit Bonnie and see how she was doing. Maybe in November....

She arrived at the supply shed, where three city trucks were parked. Her full crew should be here, as she was twenty minutes late. Sure enough, when she stepped from sun to shadow, a wall of male sweat hit her. They'd been working in the sun all day, that was certain.

Burke, her foreman, handed her a clipboard and said, "Fertilizer and pesticide applied. All trash liners filled and replaced. Bathrooms stocked. Extra help coming tomorrow. All of it."

She pretended to look at the paperwork she'd left with him

that morning. A huge checklist of everything that needed to be accomplished before the two dozen softball teams arrived. "Thanks, Burke." She glanced up and looked at all the men who'd put in full days for five solid weeks to get the sports complex looking brand new after a harsh winter. "Thank you, all."

Rae smiled. "Zack and I are buying pizza for everyone tomorrow. At the rec center. Hour-long lunches for everyone." She handed the clipboard back to Burke, who hung it on a nail by the door she'd walked through. She'd ask him about the supplies that needed refreshing after the others had left. Or maybe through a text tonight.

He handed her a single sheet of paper. "What we need to restock the shed."

She took it and let her hand fall back to her side. "Burke, do you know anything about horses?"

Confusion crossed his expression. "A bit." He watched her with his hazel eyes, something sharp there that unsettled Rae.

"Enough to help me organize a riding program?"

His eyebrows rose. "Don't we have enough to do?"

She gripped the paper a bit too tight, and the crinkling sound alerted her to her stress. She relaxed her fingers, completely overwhelmed by the many tasks that needed doing.

"Monday morning," she said, tucking the paper into the back pocket of her jeans. "Come by my office for an hour." She turned her attention to the group at large, who had finished cleaning up the shed and were waiting for five o'clock to hit.

"Go on home, guys," she said a full fifteen minutes early. Her plans to stop by the diner and get dinner for her and her mother solidified when Burke and every other male in the building hung up jackets and tool belts and keys to riding lawn mowers and left.

Only minutes later, she stood in the supply shed, glancing around at the city-owned equipment, the desk where the men turned in their timecards so they could get paid, the pegs that held shovels and rakes and extra sprinkler heads.

Loneliness descended on her in the silence that followed. She locked up and completed the loop back to her car, grateful for the blue sky and the longer evenings before darkness claimed another day.

She drove the two blocks to the rec center, which bustled with activity as townspeople came to exercise after they finished work, as the older youth volleyball program continued, as moms and little children left to head home to start dinner and get to bed.

She joined the flow of people into the building and stepped behind the desk. Down the hall, past a few doors, she finally came to her office. The youth soccer teams needed to be formed, and coaches contacted, and schedules for practices and games and tournaments made. Rae had ten days to get it all done, and she'd never completed the job faster than that.

She collected the file box containing hundreds of forms and heaved it onto her hip. If she had work to do, her mother wouldn't talk for too long about her job at the drug store, though Rae usually liked the stories. People were fascinating, and sometimes what her mother saw was stranger than fiction.

"Going home?" Meredith asked from her perch at the check-in desk.

"Going to my mother's." Rae used a dry tone that caused Meredith to chuckle. She could laugh because she had a husband and two dogs at home, waiting to fill her lonely hours with conversation and pet tricks and love.

"Have fun," Meredith singsonged. Rae had moved around the desk and was heading toward the exit when Meredith added, "Oh, and we're still on for tomorrow, right? It's salsa night for bunko."

"Cinco de Mayo was last week." Rae half-turned and smiled at her friend. Of course she hadn't forgotten about bunko, especially if there was going to be copious amounts of salsa. They'd play loud Mexican music and eat too many chips and for one night, Rae wouldn't be so lonely it choked her.

"It's the monthly theme." Meredith brushed back her blonde hair. "Denny's going to Boston for the weekend, and Layla's bringing her famous mango salsa."

"Layla better not bring another stray dog and somehow convince me to take it home with me." She already had three cats and two dogs and she had nowhere else to put another living creature.

"I will tell her no dogs." Meredith made an X in the air in front of her.

"Or cats."

"No dogs or cats. Or ferrets. No animals, period." Meredith grinned. "Can you bring your mother's almond punch?"

Rae tipped her head back and laughed. It felt good to be reminded that she *did* have friends in Island Park. She simply didn't want to go home with her friends. "You're never getting that recipe. My mom's made me promise on my grave."

A mischievous glint sparkled in Meredith's eyes. "A girl can keep trying."

Rae lifted her hand in a final farewell and left the rec center, finally feeling more like herself than she had since meeting with Ben Buttars that afternoon.

3

B en sat smashed between Sam and Logan, enduring the five miles from the farm to town with the simple hope that Rae would be at church that morning too. He'd never seen her there before, but he'd never looked. Never did much more than slip to the bench Sam dictated and lose himself inside his thoughts.

He often thought of his mother and father, of the aunt they were going to visit in Alaska when their single-engine plane went down. His mind often landed on how grateful he was for Sam for making sure they were all able to stay together.

But today, he glanced around for a certain brunette. Trouble was, women caught him looking and they looked back. He wasn't sure how long they'd been looking, but Sam had been out with several women since they'd arrive in Island Park. Logan too. Darren seemed more interested in horses than girls, and Ben had just been baking pretzels.

Now he was looking. How Sam had endured the weight of all those female eyes, Ben didn't know. He slipped down the appointed pew and took his seat against the wall, a buffer of his three brothers between him and everyone looking. It was like everyone suddenly knew that he was interested in Reagan Cantwell and had an opinion about it.

Thankfully, Sam seemed to have the timing perfected, because the pastor stood up only moments later and the service began. Halfway through the hour, Ben started to squirm. He craved wide open skies and a bustling breeze and the movement of his horse beneath his body.

He blinked, stopped scanning the backs of people's heads, and focused. Pastor Gray spoke about service and losing personal worries and cares inside helping others. "I challenge you to look at the people in your life. See if you can identify one person you could serve. Pray that opportunities to serve will be put in your life."

Ben closed his eyes, but three people had already entered his mind. Sam, the brother who'd become like a father to Ben in a single day. Missy, the only woman Ben had in his life. And Rae, the woman he *wanted* to have in his life.

He'd sat in the office for a few minutes after she'd left, wondering why she'd seemed so worried about his age. In turn, he'd been obsessed about knowing how old she was. Definitely older than him. She wore the maturity in her stature, the faint laugh lines around her eyes, the experience of speaking to men in her easy conversation.

The service ended, but Ben stayed in his seat as his brothers stood. How he'd missed the swarms of women before, he didn't know. Logan elbowed him. "You'd think there were no eligible bachelors in this town." He nodded to where Sam stood with no less than three women.

"Do you know any of them?" Ben asked, his gaze moving beyond the women to the crowd beyond, still hoping to see Rae. What he'd say to her, he had no idea. Maybe a glimpse was all he needed to make it through another week of washing horses and prepping fields and sweeping stalls.

"I think Sam likes the strawberry blonde," Darren said. "He always was a sucker for a redhead, and see how he keeps edging toward her?" Darren chuckled. "He's just gun shy after the last woman wanted to take him to Maine to meet her family after the second date."

"Who is she?" Ben watched the blonde, the interest in his brother obvious in her eyes.

"Her name's Bonnie. She works at the elementary school, I think. Her ex-husband used to own the grocery store."

"Divorced?"

Darren shrugged. "I barely get to town more than you do, Ben." He stood. "Let's go. Maybe we can get Logan and Sam out of here if we head outside."

Ben had stood and inched toward the end of the row when he spied Rae. She found him at almost the same moment, and she stilled. Ben sucked in a breath, the distance between them too great for her to notice or hear but something locked them together. Something invisible but very very real.

Then she was walking toward him, her lips curving upward and her eyes crinkling. Her black and floral skirt swished around her legs, and Ben watched the fabric, mesmerized.

"Hey," she said, glancing at Darren before meeting Ben's gaze again.

"Hey." At least he'd spoken.

Darren chuckled and kept moving, leaning in to say something to Sam as he passed. Sam immediately turned back to where Ben stood, his eyes missing nothing. What he thought, though, Ben couldn't tell.

"How was the softball tournament?" he asked.

She sighed and brushed her hair over her shoulder. She wore it down today and Ben fisted his fingers as they started to itch with the need to touch her hair.

"It was a success." She leaned into the end of the pew. "Do you—? I mean, could you come over to my office sometime this week? I've got one of my guys helping me with the riding thing and...."

Ben let her voice trail into just noise. She didn't want to work on the riding program. He'd known it from her demeanor at the farm, and now she'd given the assignment to someone else.

"Give her your number," Sam said, breaking into Ben's mounting panic.

"What?"

"She asked for your number so she could call you about the riding lessons." Sam's eyes sparkled with a tease as he extended his hand. Ben automatically reached into his pocket to retrieve his phone. Sam took it and gave it to Rae, who typed in her number and handed it back to him. Sam took hers and swiped and tapped while Ben stood there mute. He wasn't sure what coursed through him quicker, humiliation or anger. But he made no move to correct his brother, said nothing to stick up for himself. Sam had simply always been there, taking care of things for Ben. Even getting a woman's phone number.

"I'm meeting with him in the morning," Rae said. "I'll call you later."

"All right," Ben said and Rae gave him a final, foxy look before ducking her head and leaving.

"What is that about?" Sam asked, turning his back fully to the still waiting women.

"Nothing," Ben mumbled. "The riding lessons Missy put me in charge of."

"Oh, you're clearly not in charge of anything with that woman," Sam said, chuckling. "She'll chew you up and spit you out."

Ben rolled his eyes. "Like I don't know that." Inexperienced as he was with girls, even he'd known Rae didn't exist on the same playing field as he did.

"Funny thing," Sam said as they left the church. "She seemed interested."

"She did?" Ben looked at his brother. "How can you tell?"

Sam smiled, the wattage of it as bright as the sun. "I can just tell." He put his hand on Ben's arm before they go too close to where Logan and Darren waited by the truck. "You should be careful with her."

"What does that mean?"

"It means that's Reagan Cantwell. She's well-liked in Island Park, and from what I've heard, she's had her heart broken a time or two."

Ben blinked. He'd never broken a girl's heart before. He hadn't even been out on a date with someone since his parents' deaths.

Sam must've recognized the dumbfounded look on Ben's face. He slung his arm around his brother's shoulders and said, "Go slow, Ben. Be nice to her. Get to know her. See if you like her."

"What if I don't like her?"

"No big deal. If you've been nice and gone slow, no harm, no foul."

"What if I do?" Pure panic pounded through him, accelerating his pulse.

"You'll know what to do if it comes to that."

"No." Ben shook his head. "No, Sam. I have no idea what to do."

His brother laughed and opened the door to the truck. "Logan will help you."

"Help him with what?"

"Dating Reagan Cantwell." Sam climbed in the truck and slammed the door, sealing them all in the cab.

"I'm not—" Ben started, but Logan swooped in with, "*You're* dating Reagan Cantwell?" and Darren said, "You met with her once. Ben, didn't Sam advise you to go slow?"

"*He* never goes slow," Logan said, scoffing, to which Sam protested.

Ben let his brothers bicker and banter around him. At least he didn't have to talk, and his mind warped around the idea of dating Reagan Cantwell. Without any real life experience to relate it to, his fantasies ran wild through green fields with picturesque blue skies above, and they all ended right when he was about to kiss her.

———

THAT EVENING MISSY AND TUCKER ARRIVED AT THE FARM AT FIVE, just like they always did. Ben had been lying on the couch in the front room, waiting for the tell-tale rumble of Tucker's truck. When he heard it, he shot to a sitting position and then proceeded to meet them on the front porch so he could help bring in the food they'd brought.

They lived in town, but Missy brought food out to the farm every Sunday evening. She wanted to make sure the brothers ate properly at least once a week.

"Thanks, Ben." She flashed him a warm smile as she handed him a giant crock pot that smelled like roast beef. "Tucker's got the potatoes, but there's more out there." Of course there was. Missy seemed to think forty men lived in the two-story house instead of only four.

She bounded back to the truck while Ben held the door for Tucker. "She made pie," he said as he passed and strode into the kitchen with a pot the size of a watering trough.

Sam came down the hall from his bedroom, the only one on the main level, the nap he'd been taking obviously cut short if the sleepy look in his eye was any indication. "Missy need help?" he asked, running his hand through his hair and moving toward the front door at the same time.

She appeared carrying a large red bowl Ben hoped contained that frog eye salad she'd made previously. He loved that stuff.

"There's two bags of rolls," she said. "And the soda."

Ben put the meat down on the kitchen counter and reached

for a stack of real plates. Sunday was the only day of the week they didn't use paper, something Missy had insisted on. She'd claimed that her very large, very Italian family never used paper products for meals, which was a complete anomaly for Ben. After his parents' death, every meal was consumed on paper and cleaned up afterward with a simple trash bag.

Logan and Darren arrived through the back door. It had been their turn to complete the afternoon farm chores, something the brothers rotated through every other week. Ben usually napped the way Sam had, but his mind hadn't been able to switch off today.

He knew why, and it frustrated him. He longed for someone to talk to about Rae, someone who wouldn't tease him about how much he liked her after only one meeting. Someone who wouldn't spout dating advice, though Ben could certainly use it.

No, he just wanted someone to talk to, and he determined that he'd slip away from dinner early tonight and get Willow out into the woods and tell her all about the dark-haired beauty that had interrupted his life. Talking to his horse always helped, something Ben had discovered only a few months after the plane crash.

He'd been living in Montana then, on the first ranch Sam had found that would take all four brothers at the same time. For a moment, Ben missed the tall, soft-eyed owner, who'd allowed Ben to work even though he wasn't quite old enough yet. All too soon, though, the work ran out, as it had at each subsequent ranch since.

But Steeple Ridge Farm seemed like it would be the most stable. They'd been here for just over nine months, and none of their other jobs had lasted that long. As Ben dished himself the beloved frog eye salad, a sense of contentment cascaded over him like warm water. Yes, Steeple Ridge felt like the best place for Ben to put down some real roots and start living his own life.

Especially if that life included someone to share it with. Ben had never thought like that before, and he knew the reason his thoughts had started down a different path.

Rae Cantwell.

4

"Mom, that pot is boiling over." Rae watched the bubbles foam and tip over the side from her position next to the ultra-hot grill pan. She couldn't leave the fish, not if she didn't want it to overcook.

Her mom flew into action, venting the lid to reduce the boil. The scent of potato water on a hot burner filled the house, making Rae's stomach twist. She'd always hated the burnt smell of starchy water and hot metal.

Rae often spent Sunday evenings with her mom. Saturday evenings too, especially since her last break-up the previous fall. Fine, *most* evenings, if she was feeling particularly alone or needy. Which seemed to be all the time since her birthday a couple of months ago. If her mom noticed Rae's increased presence in her house, she hadn't said anything.

Rae had noticed, though. Her house seemed huge now that she could round her age up to forty. *Forty.* She'd thought she'd be married by now. Or at least have something to show for her life. But a beautiful park and a night out with friends for a Cinco de Mayo bunko night didn't seem like accomplishments.

She flipped the fish and enjoyed the sizzle of flesh against the hot pan. She'd cooked enough to know that fish should be flipped once, no more. The skin looked perfectly crispy and charred, just the way Rae liked salmon.

She preferred orzo with salmon, but her mom wanted a potato with every meal, even breakfast. Rae would just skip the potatoes, otherwise she'd feel inclined to spend an additional ten minutes on the treadmill. Which actually wouldn't be that bad, as Rae generally liked working out.

"Have you tried that sushi I told you about?" she asked as she removed the fish to a platter to rest.

Her mother wrinkled her nose. "I don't know how you eat so much fish. Especially raw." She eyed the salmon like it had done her a personal wrong, and Rae realized they were cooking two different meals. She'd eat the salmon and asparagus, and her mom would down the potatoes and maybe a single spear. Maybe.

She shook her head with a smile. They finished cooking their individual parts and served themselves their preferred foods before settling at the bar in the house Rae had grown up in. After eating, she'd wander around the backyard that was her mom's pride and joy and then head home, where the youth soccer program waited, only half-finished.

She ate, hugged her mom, and made her way home. Rae lived on the eastern edge of town, closer to the sports complex than the farm, and she paid a thirteen-year-old boy who lived down the street to keep her grass green and clipped.

Her animals waited for her on the other side of the front door, all lined up. The dogs hogged the front—mostly Beauty, the puffy white bichon who wore a perpetual smile. Her whole body wagged, and if Rae didn't greet her first, the little dog would sulk for days.

So Rae swept the dog into her arms and said, "Hey, Bee-*you*-ti-ful. Did you have a good day?" The dog never answered, but she attempted to lick Rae's face. Rae giggled and put Beauty down so she could pat her black and white shih tzu, Peaches.

The cats didn't like to be touched, so Rae simply walked past them toward their food bowls. Aloof and easily spooked, the felines just wanted to eat. "Come on, Cherry-Pop," she said, picking up the oldest cat's bowl. She fed them in the same order every morning and evening, and Cherry Popsicle had a special diet because the gray tabby cat had been overweight since Rae had adopted her.

"There you go." She set the red bowl down for Cherry-Pop, then proceeded to fill two more bowls with regular cat food for Ralph and Betty Boop, both Maine coon cats. With water bowls filled, she set about preparing a chicken and wild rice concoction for Beauty and Peaches.

She told them about the sermon from that morning, and the way her heart had jumped a little when she'd seen Ben sitting with his brothers. "They made an impressive row of men," she said, washing her hands. "I can see why every woman in town is twittering over them."

It seemed like everywhere she went—to Harry's for dinner, to The Bean for coffee, even as she walked by the elementary school —all the single girls were talking about "those Buttars brothers" out at Steeple Ridge.

Rae had stayed out of the conversations, her last relationship ending only a week before the cowboys had arrived at the farm. Only the oldest came to town very often, and Rae had no reason to spend any time with them or out on the farm.

Until now.

Ignoring her traitorous thought, she picked up her master schedule and studied it. But her mind circled back to Ben Buttars and his sweet smile, his nervous demeanor. Only by absorbing herself in the work of organizing the six-year-old teams could she eradicate him from her mind.

———

THE NEXT MORNING, RAE BLASTED HER SEVENTIES ROCK WHILE SHE showered and got dressed. While she pulled her hair into a ponytail and laced her tennis shoes. While she put peanut butter granola in yogurt and gathered together all the soccer materials.

The music soothed her, though it was at least ten decibels louder than a safe listening limit. She needed the noise to clear her head, to prepare herself to go to work with mostly men. Sometimes the overload of testosterone was exhausting by nine-fifteen, and she didn't have to be to work until nine o'clock.

She looped her purse over her shoulder and armed herself with her gigantic water bottle. "House, turn—" She went mute when the music should have, because she came face-to-face with Ben, who stood next to the couch, watching her with a look of pure amusement on his handsome face.

She squeaked, the sound thankfully covered by the still-blasting rock song. He lifted his eyebrows, his face breaking into a full smile.

"What are you doing here?" she yelled. Foolishness spiked through her and she said, "House, turn off the music." Her smart house silenced, leaving only awkwardness in the air between her and Ben.

"I knocked," he said. "A few times. Even tried the doorbell." His eyes sparkled like brown diamonds, and she took a step toward him.

"Did you need something?" She didn't need to be embarrassed, but she hadn't felt this self-conscious in a man's presence for a while. She reached up and touched her ponytail, wishing she'd left her hair down this morning. And maybe curled it.

Ridiculous, she thought. She only took such care with her appearance for church, and sometimes not even then. But going to work in a cement box, wearing jeans and sneakers most of the time, didn't require makeup or curling irons or fancy conditioner.

"Missy sent me to town to get something she forgot," he said.

"Wanted me to stop by and give it to you." He extended something toward her though they stood at least fifteen feet apart.

"What is it?" Rae closed the distance between them and took the half-size envelope she hadn't noticed him holding.

"I don't know," Ben said. "She insisted you needed it before you went to work this morning."

He didn't seem super-thrilled to have driven into town to make sure she got the envelope, and Rae had no idea what it could contain. It felt hard, and small, like a credit card. She swallowed, unsure if she should open it in front of Ben. Would he expect her to read the card out loud?

She glanced at him, confused at the way her heart pitter-patted like she was an eighteen-year-old schoolgirl infatuated with the latest rodeo champion who'd ridden into town. With her attention back on the envelope, heat rushed into her face. She was *attracted* to Ben Buttars, and with the way her face flamed, everyone within Island Park city limits would know.

"I think your cat is trying to escape," he said.

She pulled her fingers away from the flap and searched for the offending feline. "Grab him," she said when she spotted Ralph making a beeline past Ben's legs.

He bent to grab the animal but missed. Rae abandoned her purse, the water bottle, and the envelope and hurried after the cat. "He doesn't have claws," she said, a note of anxiety in her voice. "And he's half-deaf. He really can't leave the house." She arrived on the front porch to an empty yard, the cat already gone.

5

"Ralph," Ben called for the thirtieth time. The little cat had really hunkered down. He wasn't under the porch, or in the window wells. Rae didn't have many other hiding places in the front yard. No wheelbarrows or lawn decorations. Everything was straight and neat, just like the interior of her house. She was organized and controlled in all things—except her animals.

As she searched for the coon cat named Ralph, she wore tension in the lines around her mouth and worry rode in her delightful eyes. Ben wanted to be the one to fix everything for her, a thought which surprised and scared him. He'd never been able to fix anything, for anyone. No, Sam took care of all family things. Darren made sure the laundry got done. Logan paid their bills. And Ben baked pretzels.

Remembering his desire to start to live his own life, he rounded the corner of the house to find three pine trees creating a natural fence between Rae's house and her neighbor's. A flash of gray and black fur caught his eye, and he spotted the cat cowering next to the trunk of a particularly bushy pine.

"Rae," he called, inching closer to the tree without spooking the cat. She appeared at the edge of the house, and he nodded. "He's down there."

"I'll grab him a treat." She left as fast as she'd arrived, and Ben slid his foot another six inches closer to the tree.

He'd crouched at the edge of the longest pine boughs when she returned. "Chicken," she said, passing him a large chunk of cooked meat.

Ben held it out, and Ralph's pointed, peaked ears twitched. He focused on the chicken, but he didn't so much as move a paw a centimeter forward.

"C'mon," Ben cooed to the cat. "C'mon now." He kept his emotions even, the way he did when he worked with a horse that had a nervous personality. He stretched the treat further under the tree, and Ralph's nose quivered.

The cat took a step forward, and Ben employed his patience. Rae started to say something, but Ben silenced her with a slow shake of his head. "C'mon." He held the chicken perfectly still, waiting for Ralph to take one more step.

Just one...more...step. The cat moved, and Ben dove. Pine needles scraped the side of his face and up his arm as he gripped the cat and hauled him out. Ralph mewed as Ben stood. He allowed the cat his treat and stroked his soft fur. He definitely wasn't an outdoor cat.

"You have a lot of cats?" he asked.

"Three," she said, stepping into his personal space and running her fingers down the cat's head and back too. Her skin touched his, and lightning sparked up his arm and into his heart. He sucked in a breath and looked at her.

Their eyes locked, and everything around them fell away. He couldn't feel the spring morning air. Couldn't smell the pine tree only steps from him. Couldn't detect the weight of the cat in his arms.

"You're beautiful," he whispered, the words coming from

nowhere and sliding across his vocal chords before he could tell himself to keep the thought private.

She blinked, but surely she'd been told such a sentiment dozens of times. A smile enhanced her beauty, and Ben found a blush in her cheeks when she said, "Thanks, Ben."

He passed Ralph to her, and she turned away and took the cat back inside the house. He stayed outside, needing the cool temperatures to calm himself down. Somehow he knew that telling Rae she was beautiful only the third time they'd interacted wasn't going slow. Wasn't being careful, the way Sam had advised.

Maybe Sam's not right about everything, Ben thought. And telling a woman she was beautiful *was* nice, and Sam had said to be nice too.

Rae pulled the front door closed behind her and kept her eyes on his as she approached him. "I should have something ready with the riding program for you to review by, say...Friday?"

"Sure, Friday," Ben said. "I have your number."

"I'll let you know what time." She grinned up at him and opened her car door. She set her belongings inside and turned back to the house. "Well, I have to get my file box. I'll see you later?"

Ben realized he'd followed her right up to the car, and she couldn't actually move around him. Heat flooded his face, and he practically fell down in his haste to put some distance between them. "See you later," he confirmed and headed to Sam's truck, which he'd parked behind her car. As he drove away, a text came in.

From Missy: *Did you catch Rae before she left for work?*

"Sure did," he dictated into his phone and hit send.

Did you talk to her?

As Ben lifted the phone to his lips to reply in the affirmative, he realized he'd been set up. Missy had *set him up*!

"What was in that envelope?" he dictated and sent.

Missy didn't respond, only confirming Ben's suspicions.

"Are you telling me I didn't need to drive into town this morning?"

The minutes and miles rolled by in silence, and when he returned to Steeple Ridge, he found Missy's horse gone from the barn, gone from the pastures, gone gone gone.

He shook his head, but a smile slipped across his face. So he'd wasted an hour. He'd gotten to see Rae dancing around to that awful rock music, and that was worth being a bit behind in his chores.

————

"Is Rae going to take on the horseback riding lessons?"

Ben turned to find Missy leaning against the fence, her auburn hair being lifted by the breeze.

"I haven't heard." He also didn't know the possibility of her passing on the lessons even existed. He swallowed and kept a tight grip on the reins of the three horses he'd been leading toward the back barn. "She's really busy with the youth soccer program right now."

Missy cocked her head to the side, her eyes full of sparkle. "She loves her soccer program."

Ben had no idea what that meant, but maybe Rae liked her community sports programs the way he liked riding his horse through the woods.

"You went over the proposal I prepared?"

"Page by page," he said. "She seemed impressed."

Missy waggled her phone. "She was." She giggled and the grin didn't leave her face. "By you."

Ben held very still. "I don't know what you mean."

"I know you don't."

Ben liked Missy; always had. "Missy," he started. "I have no— uh—dating experience."

"I'm sure you—"

"No," Ben interrupted. "None. The last girl I went out with was fifteen years old. *I* was fifteen years old."

She blinked, sobering as she realized that Ben had spoken true. He shifted his feet but held his ground. He employed the well of bravery he'd been storing up for a decade and didn't look away from Missy. "I need help."

"Maybe Sam—"

"If Sam knew what he was doing, he'd have a girl of his own by now." Immediate regret filled him, and he sighed out his frustration. "I didn't mean that. Sam's great. I just—" He glanced at one of the horses when it nickered. "I like Rae."

"She likes you too." Missy stepped forward and put her hand on Ben's forearm. "You don't have to know what you're doing. You like her. She likes you. Maybe you just go get something to eat and talk."

Ben nodded, because that sounded good. Getting dinner sounded like a real date. He vaguely remembered taking girls to get ice cream at the grocery store back in Wyoming.

"So do I text her...or call...?" The thought of waiting for Rae to pick up his call sent terror right to through his chest. "And what are we supposed to talk about?"

Missy laughed and walked toward the barn, where he found Tucker loitering in the doorway. "You'll figure it out," she called over her shoulder.

He was so tired of everyone telling him that.

———

Tuesday blurred into Wednesday, which dawned into Thursday. Ben hadn't heard anything from Rae, and the week was almost over. He finished in the outer pastures by mid-afternoon and returned to the house to make a batch of soft pretzels.

While setting fences and repairing rungs, he'd decided he

wasn't going to wait any longer. He knew where Rae worked, and he knew where she lived, and he knew she liked his pretzels.

Armed with four warm treats, he swung by the grocery store and bought a fresh bottle of gourmet mustard before texting from the safety of the truck. *Are you home? Or still at work?*

Her answer came back in seconds. *On my way home now.*

Call me when you get there?

Sure.

Ben exhaled, his muscles releasing that she hadn't denied him or ignored him. When she called only two minutes later, he asked, "Am I all right to swing by? I made pretzels."

She laughed, the sound making his insides soft and a smile to come to his face. "How can I refuse pretzels when they're delivered by a cute cowboy?"

"What if it was just the cute cowboy?" Ben asked.

Rae quieted, and Ben cursed himself for letting his thoughts slip out of his mouth uncensored. "Oh, did you bring Sam with you?" Rae asked, a heavy teasing note in her voice.

"No," Ben said. "He likes blondes. And he can't even make toast without burning it."

Rae giggled again. "Well, I guess you'll have to come by yourself."

"I'm not coming alone. I have this gourmet mustard that has your name written all over it." He pulled onto the street and pointed his truck east. The houses increased in size as he drove, as Rae told him about her mom and asked if he'd eaten dinner.

When he confessed he hadn't, she said, "The only place that delivers is Pizza Palace. Is that okay?"

"Have you ever met a man who doesn't like pizza?" He turned onto her street and found her sitting on her steps three houses down on the left.

"Yes, actually." Her hair flowed over her shoulders and she tucked it behind her ear as he pulled into her driveway.

"I don't know if I believe that." He collected the pretzels and the condiments he'd bought and got out of the truck. He pulled the phone from his ear, thrilled he'd figured out how to flirt over the phone. And it hadn't been too terribly hard.

He approached the steps, where she stood to receive him. "He was lactose intolerant," she said. "Let's just say we ate out very little."

He handed her the plate of pretzels. "I love cheese. All kinds of cheese."

She eyed the ketchup. "And ketchup."

"You know what's delicious?" He started up her steps. "Cheddar with ketchup."

"Stop it."

He opened the door and was met with a row of two dogs followed by a line of three cats. "No, really," he said, bending down to pat the fluffy white dog. He turned back to her. "Ketchup is a universal condiment. It goes with everything."

"That is not true."

"Name one thing you can't put ketchup on."

She closed the door behind him, the lemony sugary scent of her house overwhelming his senses. "Ice cream."

He turned and peered down at her, the corners of his mouth twitching upward. "Done it. Delicious."

Horror passed through her expression, followed quickly by disbelief.

"It's like tomato jam."

"Ketchup is about as far from tomato jam as you can get," she said. "I know. My mother makes it every year from the tomatoes she grows herself."

He backed up a step and lifted his free hand in defeat. "You keep having your boring hot fudge on your sundae."

Her laughter joined him in the kitchen. Her body heat penetrated his when she stepped right into his personal space and scrolled on her phone. "What kind of pizza do you like?"

He glanced down at her. "Whatever you like."

She nudged him with her shoulder, and Ben enjoyed her proximity, the sound of her voice as she read from the menu, the way he felt comfortable in her house. In fact, Ben felt like today was the first day of a brand new life for him. A life beyond his brothers. A life beyond farm work.

A real life.

6

R ae flirted shamelessly, glad when Ben finally seemed
to notice. His smile came quickly and he kept himself
close to her while she ate half a pretzel and ordered
pizza.

"Have you had that pizza with the pretzel crust?" she asked.

He took a ketchup-laden bite of pretzel and shook his head.

"Comes with cheese sauce instead of pizza sauce. My ex—"
She sucked in a breath, cursing herself for speaking. But come
on. It wasn't like she wouldn't have ex-boyfriends. At least she
didn't have any ex-husbands to detail.

"My ex loved it," she said. "They don't have it here in Island
Park. You have to drive up to Burlington."

"We should do that sometime." He finished his pretzel and
moved into her living room, his gorgeous eyes soaking up the art
she'd framed and hung on the walls. It provided a splash of color
among the beige, gray, and cream color scheme.

"Pizza should be here in twenty minutes," she said, moving a
throw pillow—another way she'd added a touch of color and
personality—and settling into the corner of her couch. Beauty

immediately jumped into her lap and sat, her little face toward Ben as if to say, *She's mine.*

Rae smiled as she patted Beauty's head. "Do you have any pets?"

"We have a dog, but it's really Logan's." He joined her on the couch, not too close, not too far. She wondered what his dating history was, but she wouldn't be asking. It would come out. She had a feeling Ben had a lot to say, bottled up deep down inside him.

"The dog is Logan's, but most everything else is Sam's." He gestured toward the driveway. "That truck. The credit for us getting jobs."

Rae gazed at him, trying to find the meaning behind his words. "Why's that?"

Ben shrugged and let his hands hang between his knees. "He's the oldest. Wanted to keep us together."

"Keep you together after what?"

Ben swallowed; the movement in his throat looked painful. "After our parents died. I was only fifteen."

Rae's heart bled a little. She reached out and touched her hand to his forearm. A snapple, razzle, pop raced up her arm, originating from the warmth of his skin. He stared at her fingers, but she couldn't read his expression.

"I'm sorry," Rae said. "Both of them?"

Nodding, Ben let the story spill from his lips. "They were going to visit my aunt Annie in Alaska. She was about to have her first baby, and she was my mom's youngest sister. Sam's older than her." Ben chuckled, and the sound actually held notes of happiness. "They had to take a single-engine plane from Anchorage out to where my aunt lived. It crashed. All seven people on board died."

"That's terrible." She shifted and her fingers slipped in between his. "How long has it been?"

"Just over ten years," he said. "Sam took good care of us.

Logan and Darren—they're twins—they'd just graduated from high school in Wyoming, where we lived. Sam was working a ranch in Montana, and he came back to get us all. Took us up there. We worked there for a few months before moving on. We've been all over the west, and now we're here." He squeezed her fingers and looked up into her face. "I like it here."

A smile spread her lips, and she leaned toward him the slightest bit. It might as well have been a lunge for the way it made Rae's heart ricochet around her chest.

"Have you lived here a long time?" he asked, his voice only slightly scratched.

"Yeah." She nodded. "Born and raised. My mom still lives over by the high school on the south side of town." Her smile faded the longer he gazed at her. Rae had had boyfriends look at her with the same softness Ben radiated from his. It made her feel beautiful, and desirable, and so much less lonely.

"I'm glad you like it here," she said. A moment later, the doorbell rang and she startled, her eyes flying to the door. "Must be the pizza." She flew into motion, answering the door and paying for the food and laughing with the delivery driver, a high school senior who'd reffed her soccer games for years.

She shut the door and walked into the kitchen, noticing that Ben hadn't so much as moved an inch. "You gonna come eat?" she asked, pulling a stack of paper plates from the cupboard.

He stood and joined her in the kitchen and took three pieces of the all-meat pie she'd ordered. "Next time, I'm paying," he said.

Rae blinked at him a couple of times before saying, "All right, Ben. Next time, you pay." Giddy he'd made it clear there would be a next time, she gathered two pieces of pizza for herself.

"Next time, maybe we could go out." He sat at her kitchen counter and bit into his pizza. "Do you like to eat out?"

"Remember how I went out with that guy who was lactose intolerant? Yeah, that didn't last long." She sat next to him, taking in the intoxicating smell of leather and sandalwood, along with the warmth of his welcome company.

Rae suspected he didn't have to say much during meal times, what with three older brothers and all. So she said, "Tell me about some of the ranches where you've worked."

And as he started with the Spring Creek Horse facility in Nevada, she basked in the deep timbre of his voice, the rumble of it infusing her chest and worming its way into her heart.

———

"You have a visitor." Meredith leaned in the doorway of Rae's office.

Rae barely glanced up from the field map she was moments away from finishing. "Just a sec."

"It's one of those Buttars brothers. Tall, dark, dreamy? Said he had an appointment."

Rae's pen stuttered across the page, leaving a dotted line where there shouldn't be one. "He's not supposed to be here until four." She glanced at her phone, which read one-thirty, and stared at Meredith.

"He's carrying a brown paper bag from the diner." Meredith wore a smile reminiscent of the Cheshire Cat. "I think he wants to steal you away for lunch."

That sounded absolutely heavenly to Rae, and her pulse thrummed out several extra beats. She was glad Meredith couldn't see or hear her heartbeat. She swept back an errant wisp of hair that had come loose from her ponytail at some point that morning. She'd been at the Sports Complex for hours, gearing up for the second round of the softball tournament. And since Burke had pulled the double shift last Friday night, Rae was on the clock for tonight.

The work was easy; she'd just make sure the bathrooms

stayed stocked and keep an eye on the facilities. But it was another six hours of work past five o'clock.

Her stomach roared, taking that moment to remind her that she hadn't eaten yet. She had no idea what Ben might order for her, and she really wanted to find out.

"His name's Ben," she said to Meredith. "You can send him back."

Meredith didn't just turn and head down the hall to the reception desk. She entered the office and sat in the single chair in front of Rae's desk. "His name's Ben? You think I don't know? Everyone in town knows their names."

Rae rolled her eyes. She'd stayed out of this gossip for a reason. Ben hadn't seemed surprised that she didn't know the story about how he and his brothers had come to Island Park, but in most other situations, she would've known. She would've had her relationship eyes on the four brothers the first week they'd arrived in town.

A surge of bitterness coated the back of her throat when she thought about why she hadn't been infatuated with the Buttars brothers.

Damian Dallas.

She hated thinking about Damian, because it reminded her of how much she'd given him only to have her heart shredded and strung out along Main Street for all to see. At least he'd left town. At least she didn't have to worry about running into him when she picked up dinner or did her grocery shopping. At least he'd been gone before Ben showed up.

"Can you just send him back?" Rae asked, focusing on her map again.

"Are you seeing him?"

"Yes." Rae lifted her eyes to her friend's. "He has an appointment."

Meredith tipped her head back and laughed, her honey-blonde hair falling over her shoulders. "All right, Rae. Whatever you say." She stood and disappeared out of the office.

Rae's heart hammered. Though she kept her pen steady and finished the map, inside, she felt like someone had unloosed a herd of wild antelope and they were leaping frantically.

She stood and moved to the door just as Ben arrived. "Hey, there." He beamed down on her and the temperature in the entire rec center lifted at least ten degrees.

Rae took a deep breath of Ben, his cologne so delicious her mouth almost started watering. "Hey, yourself. I just have to run this over to my secretary so she can get started on it."

Ben squeezed past her and set the brown paper sack on her desk. "I'll come with you."

"It's two doors down." She entered the hall with Ben's cowboy boots clomping along behind her. "I finished the map and the schedule," she said over her shoulder. She ducked into April's office and found the woman leaning against the wall, stretching.

"Foot giving you trouble again?" Rae asked.

April groaned as she leaned further into the wall. "This plantar fasciitis is no joke." She hobbled back to her desk. "And there's no treatment. Well, besides the stretching and ice and painkill—" Her gaze landed on Ben on the last word, and her voice fell into silence.

"I finished the schedule for the youth soccer." Rae set the folder on April's desk. April, who was running her fingers through her light brown hair. "And the map of the fields for each week. I need you to get the packets ready for the coaches." She glanced at Ben and back to April.

"Yes, coaches," April said, pressing her lips together, her eyes solely for Ben.

"Have you met Ben Buttars?" Rae asked, moving back to where Ben loitered in the doorway. "He's working with me to start a horseback riding program out at Steeple Ridge Farm."

April stood and leaned her weight into her palms against the desk. "Do you have time for that? I could take that on...."

Rae smiled, the action a little stickier than she liked. "You already work ten extra hours a week. I saw you in here last weekend."

"Which means *you* were here last weekend too."

Rae grinned at her assistant and long-time friend. April had been doing her job twice as long as Rae, and she'd really shown her the ropes when Rae stepped into this role.

"Which one of you has more experience with horses?" Ben asked, stepping into the conversation. Stepping right to Rae's side. She half-expected him to take her hand in his, and she stiffened.

"Oh, fine." April sat down. "Rae wins that one. Probably has all the medals in her living room."

Rae cringed inwardly and faced Ben as he turned toward her. "Medals?"

She grabbed his arm. "Soccer stuff is due by the end of the day Tuesday. I have to get it out to coaches on Wednesday." She towed Ben out of April's office and back to hers.

"Medals?" he said again once she closed the door.

He half-sat on her desk while she leaned against the door, his eyes sparkling with mischief and amusement. And maybe something more that Rae couldn't identify.

"I used to show horses," she said. "Satisfied?"

"Absolutely not," he said.

Rae laughed, and the awkwardness in the office dissipated. "It was a long time ago."

"Doesn't mean we can't talk about it." He pushed off the desk and took a slow step toward her. "Or that you can't show me the medals." He approached her, making her breath catch in her throat. "Or that I don't want to see you in the saddle again." He licked his lips, invaded her personal space, and threaded his fingers through hers.

She sucked in a breath at the intimacy of his touch and tilted her head back to maintain eye contact. "Maybe," she said.

His eyebrows shot toward his hairline. "Maybe?"

"It was a *long* time ago. I stopped showing when I was seventeen."

"How many years ago was that?"

"Are you asking me how old I am?"

"You asked me first."

"I figured it out." Rae grinned up at him, relieved that he was four years older than her required twenty-one.

"Someone as smart as you can figure anything out." The husky quality of his voice set Rae's nerve endings on fire.

"Yes, well, I haven't been on a horse in eighteen years." She gave his hands a squeeze and slipped away from him, the nearness of him, the sensual touch, the way her fantasies had started spiraling toward kissing him all just a little bit too much to be contained in her office.

To her relief, he didn't run screaming from her office once he knew she was a whole decade older than him. He simply sat in the chair across from her desk and reached for the paper bag, a hint of a blush in his face.

7

"I brought you a triple cheese grilled cheese," Ben said, his mind still turning over the fact that she was thirty-five. That was even older than Sam. With a bolt of realization as hot and fast as lightning, Ben worried that she'd be more interested in Sam than him.

"From Harry's?" she asked.

"Yes, ma'am." He passed her the paper-wrapped sandwich, along with a bag of French fries. "He said you liked the sweet potato fries."

"So you asked him what I liked." She unwrapped the sandwich, looking up at him from under her lashes.

"Of course," he said. "I didn't want to show up with something you're allergic to or whatever." Ben squirmed on the inside but made sure his muscles didn't so much as twitch—something he'd seen Sam do when he talked to women. He seemed so cool, so collected. Ben tried to imitate that, but showing up a few hours early for his appointment was already a risk. He hadn't wanted to mess up the food too.

Now, as he watched Rae, he couldn't help feeling like he'd made a mistake by asking Harry what Rae Cantwell liked for lunch. "He had a lot of options," Ben said, hoping the conversation would erase his anxiety. "You must eat at Harry's a lot."

"Define 'a lot'," she said with a flirtatious giggle that sent heat straight through Ben.

"More than me," he said.

"How many times have you eaten there?"

"This would be the third time."

Rae froze with half of her sandwich near her mouth. "Three times? You've eaten at the diner three times in nine months?"

He took a bite of his turkey club and chewed, a smile almost exploding onto his face once he swallowed. "You know I've lived at Steeple Ridge for nine months?"

"Every woman without a diamond on her left hand knows how long you boys have been in town." Rae rolled her eyes, but a laugh—pure and loud and absolutely freeing—burst from Ben's mouth. He hadn't laughed like that in a long time. Maybe a decade. Maybe even before his parents' deaths.

Rae watched him with an edge in her eyes that Ben liked. He finally quieted and took another bite of his sandwich.

"My older brothers date," he said once he'd finished the club. "Me and Darren, well, we haven't gotten off the farm much."

She brushed the crumbs from her fingers and wiped her mouth. "We'll have to change that."

"Are you free for dinner tonight?" he asked, surprised at how easily the words came to him. How smoothly they'd slid from his throat.

Disappointment cut through her beautiful, warm, brown eyes. "I'm working the softball tournament tonight."

Ben nodded, a sharp slice of displeasure moving through him too. "What does that entail?"

"Someone from the city has to be on-site," she explained. "I oversee the entire facility, and my foreman did it last weekend. It's my turn."

"I imagine the tournament will go pretty late."

"Usually about eleven. Then I have to make sure everything gets restocked and cleaned up, make sure those lights get shut off. I'll be lucky to get home by midnight. It'll probably be closer to one."

Ben nodded, pushing his hat lower over his eyes. He wished he could switch the topic to something else, but he didn't know how. "So breakfast tomorrow is out."

"I hardly ever eat breakfast anyway," Rae said, bringing Ben's head back up.

"No breakfast?"

"I never have time."

"Is that why you're eating lunch at two o'clock?"

"I'm eating lunch at two o'clock because that's when you brought it."

Ben blinked and stared, unsure if she was flirting or not. He'd asked the blonde at the front desk if Rae had eaten yet, and she'd said no. Who didn't eat breakfast and then skipped lunch too?

He returned his attention to his potato chips, at a complete loss in the conversation now.

"But I could go to dinner tomorrow night," Rae said, throwing him a life preserver.

He grabbed onto it and held it tight. "Oh, yeah? What time?" He was on weekend chores, but he could potentially switch with Darren or Logan if he confessed it was the only time he could take Rae to dinner. He thought he could put up with a bit of teasing if it meant he could hold her hand and sit across from her while they shared a meal.

"Anytime," she said. "I don't normally work on Saturday."

"April seemed to think you did."

"Summer is my busiest time," she said, pulling another folder toward her. "So let's get started on the horseback riding stuff." She glanced at him, all playfulness gone. Funny thing was, he liked this take-charge, all-business version of Rae almost as much as the flirty, fun version of her.

———

"WHERE HAVE YOU BEEN ALL DAY?" SAM ASKED AS SOON AS BEN stepped into the farmhouse. He set the three pizza boxes he'd brought from town on the kitchen counter.

"Town," he said. Nothing more. Sam had never overly detailed his lady friends, what they did, where they went. Ben didn't see the need for him to do so either. "I brought dinner since it's my turn."

"You've been gone since noon." Sam seemed determined to be in a bad mood.

Ben sighed and decided to come clean. "I had a meeting with Rae Cantwell about the horseback riding lessons."

His brother grunted, and Ben opened the lids on the pizza boxes and got out the paper plates. He texted his brothers, who showed up five minutes later. They came in with loud voices and laughter, eliminating the silence between Sam and Ben.

After everyone had washed up, Sam swiped his cowboy hat from his head. "Ben's gonna say grace tonight."

Ben thanked the Lord for family, for their jobs, that they had enough money for food and fun, for their house that kept them warm in the winter and cool in the summer. He expressed his gratitude for horses and Vermont and Tucker and Missy and Steeple Ridge. He finished his prayer, and everyone started for the food.

Sam picked up a slice and didn't look at Ben when he asked, "You went to see Rae?"

"Yeah," Ben said, unable to deny it. He'd already said he met with her that afternoon. "Don't worry. I'm going slow."

"Oh yeah? Is your definition of slow going over to her place mid-week?" He picked up a paper place. "Twice?"

"Missy sent me on Tuesday," Ben said, his defenses all the way up. "She totally set me up. I don't even know what was in that envelope, but I'm certain I didn't need to drive it over there first thing."

A smile flickered across his face, but he ironed it flat real fast. "Missy can meddle sometimes."

"I went on Thursday because I was tired of waiting to hear from her," Ben admitted. "Was that wrong?"

"If it was, you would've known." Sam opened the third box to find the Hawaiian pizza and took four slices now, Ben's answers apparently spurring his appetite.

"How?"

"She wouldn't have asked you to stay for dinner, and she would've thrown you from her office this afternoon."

"How did you know she asked me to stay for dinner?"

"This town has twelve thousand people in it," he said. "I can find out pretty much anything I want with a couple of texts." He gave Ben a pointed look. "So behave yourself."

Ben took the combination pizza, or the last two pieces left by Logan. "Behave myself? You realize the last girl I went out with was fifteen years old, right?"

Sadness crossed Sam's expression. "I know, Ben. This is good for you." He grinned and headed for the back yard, where the brothers normally ate at a picnic table on the patio when the weather was good. "Just...think if you'd want Mom to know what you're doing with Rae. If not, don't do that." He bumped his way through the door, leaving Ben with those words.

Ben cracked ice into a glass and filled it with water. So maybe he liked Rae because she was paying attention to him. Was that the worst thing in the world? He liked her laugh too, and the scent of her skin, and her attention to detail.

He was intrigued by the fact that she'd shown horses, and he wanted to see those medals and hear those stories. She hadn't given the horseback riding lessons to someone else at the rec center, though she already had a very full plate, though April had offered. That meant something, right?

She'd let him hold her hand, and Ben stared out the window as the memory of her fingers in his zinged along his palm.

"You comin'?" Sam called, launching Ben from his fantasies and toward the reality of the back yard. He could usually make it through a meal without speaking, but as he took his spot at the picnic table, he endured the weight of all three of his brother's eyes and he knew the questions would start before he'd taken his first bite of dinner.

"You kiss her yet?" Logan asked with a huge smile, and Ben sighed before stuffing half a slice of pizza into his mouth.

―――――

Dawn found Ben walking through the woods, Willow's reins in his hand. Out here, everything seemed clear. Out here, he didn't care that he might've come on too strong with Rae. Out here, he could breathe.

He parked himself against a tree trunk and let Willow graze in a meadow of fresh grass. As the gray morning got warmed and lit by the sun, Ben's spirits turned gold too. Rae was thirty-five years old. If she didn't want to eat the grilled cheese sandwich he'd brought her, she wouldn't.

She hadn't seemed to mind holding his hand, and he hadn't been so clueless as to do it in front of her secretary or anyone else. He'd definitely let her dictate when she wanted to take the relationship public.

A grin danced across his face. *The relationship.*

Fear and joy seized his muscles at the same time. Maybe he really was being too hasty, already using labels he shouldn't even be thinking.

He exhaled as he got to his feet and collected Willow's reins. "Have I told you about Rae?" he asked the horse as he led her through the meadow. "Of course I have. She's nice, though, and she let me hold her hand in her office. The door was closed, but."

Ben lifted one shoulder in a shrug and kept plodding through the forest. His horse came with him, never questioning him, never teasing him, never rolling her eyes but not saying anything. She did sigh a couple of times, but Willow always did.

Eventually Ben trotted the horse back to the farm and tied her in the washing stalls. After she was dry and brushed out, he put her in the pasture closest to the farmhouse and went inside to find breakfast.

One of his brothers had set out several boxes of cereal, along with a gallon of milk. No one else sat at the counter or the dining room table, and Ben didn't know if they'd already eaten or not.

He had chores to do with the boarded horses, but they would keep for another ten minutes. At least that was what he'd tell Sam if he got criticized for his early-morning walk through the woods. Show his brother what it felt like to be on the receiving end of "It'll keep."

He ate two bowls of sugary, marshmallowy cereal without encountering anyone. He found himself wishing one of his brothers would come in, but they didn't. Ben would've taken Missy or Tucker, and they were always around on the weekend. But today, they weren't. It seemed as though Steeple Ridge was deserted.

Dust kicked up under his boots as he walked toward the back barn. He set his muscles to work, the only way he knew how to free his mind. He fed horses. He watered horses. He led horses to their assigned pastures.

After a while of working, Sam found him cleaning out the horse stalls. "How close are you to finishing?"

"Couple of hours," Ben said. He hadn't told anyone about his dinner date with Rae that night. He didn't want to add any more fuel to their fire, and the easiest way to do that was to put his head down and take their ribbing until they'd got bored.

"It's Missy's birthday." Sam knocked on the stall next to him. "We're headed into town for lunch and then we're gonna attempt to find her a birthday present. Then we're going to dinner at her parents' house in Burlington."

If Sam said "then" one more time, Ben's head was going to explode. How had he forgotten about Missy's birthday? Tucker had been telling them about it for at least two months.

"Ben?"

"Right," Ben practically barked. "Missy. Birthday. Burlington." He dug the pitchfork into the straw with vigor.

"What's wrong?"

"Nothing." He didn't want to tell his brother about his date. He'd been hoping to sneak away with a fresh shave, a fresh set of clothes, and a fresh opportunity to get to know Rae better.

"This have anything to do with Rae?" Sam spoke kindly, his voice low and brotherly.

"Nope." He'd cleaned out the stall in record time.

"She's called three times."

Ben's movement stumbled, and he tried to cover it up. He desperately wanted to pat his back pocket and find his phone, but he knew he wouldn't. He must've left it in the kitchen at breakfast.

Stupid, he chastised himself. *Stupid, stupid, stupid.*

He met Sam's eyes, and found laughter and kindness in them. He'd dated a fair bit, but no one teased him all the time. In that moment, Ben realized that his brothers were teasing him because Ben dating anyone was new for them too.

"Did you answer?" he asked, almost dreading the answer.

"Logan wanted to, but I managed to get to the phone first." Sam held it up and twirled it in his hands. "You owe me big time. He wanted to make kissy noises as a hello."

Ben couldn't believe the immaturity of his older brothers. "It's no wonder none of us are married."

Sam laughed and handed Ben his phone. "Call her back. Invite her to dinner if you want."

"With Missy's family?" Pure panic pounded through his veins.

"All she ever says about them is how loud they are and how many of them there are. Why would I want to bring Rae along to that?"

Sam shrugged, a twinkle in his eye Ben could see even through the shadows in the barn. "It's a half-hour drive there and a half-hour back."

"We have one truck among the four of us."

"We'll ride with Tucker and Missy."

Ben shook his head, his mind racing, pacing, chasing. All of these arrangements would require explanations. Explanations he didn't want to give. "No, it's fine. I'll call her and set up something else. Go slow, like you said."

Too bad everything inside him wanted to push on the accelerator. Push it all the way to the floor. See how fast he could go. He'd never felt anything like it. Everything was new and exciting and wonderful, and he wanted to breathe it in, let it fill him up, show him how to live.

He hadn't realized he wasn't living before now. And he didn't want—no, he *wouldn't*—go back to the ghost of a person he'd been before he'd met Rae.

8

"It's totally okay." Rae collapsed onto her couch, half disappointed and half relieved that Ben couldn't get together for dinner tonight. A sigh escaped her mouth. "Now I don't have to shower." She smiled, hoping the gesture would infuse into her words. Of course she'd known Missy's birthday was in May. She'd just forgotten.

"What's your schedule like next week?" he asked.

She sighed and lay down on her couch. "I don't know. I'll check it tomorrow night and text you." She didn't want to think about her schedule on the weekends. And now she had an entire Saturday night free. A week ago, she would've been depressed about the possibility of spending a weekend evening with her mother. Or by herself.

But now, that didn't matter. Rae actually craved a night in, and after she hung up with Ben, she rolled onto her side and flipped on the television. The past few weeks had caught up to her, and combined with last night's late hour at the Sports Complex, she'd slept until mid-morning.

"All right," Ben said in his Wyoming cowboy drawl. "I'll see you later then."

Rae hung up and stared at the soundless pictures on the TV. She needed to eat, and maybe get her friend a birthday gift, then she could fall asleep on the sofa if she wanted. So she heaved herself back to sitting put on her shoes again. She lived about six blocks from Main Street and all the shopping. And if there was anything worth doing on a Saturday night by herself, it was shopping.

Her long strides ate up the distance to the thoroughfare of Island Park, and she relaxed at the familiar sight of the government buildings that sat at the end of Main Street. The police station, fire station, and courthouse marked the beginning of the commercial district of town.

The scent of pizza wafted toward her, but she bypassed the Pizza Palace and continued on toward the department store, hardware store, and cutesy boutiques that lined the street a few blocks down.

She detoured into Paige's clothing boutique, already knowing she'd probably come out with something for herself rather than for Missy.

"Hey, Rae." Paige glanced over from where she fussed over a mannequin. "How are you?" She left her work to give Rae a hug. "I haven't seen you in a while."

"I bought so much last time I was in here, I haven't needed anything new." The last time Rae had gone shopping had been the weekend after her break-up with Damian. She'd spent way too much money in an attempt to soothe the fact that the man had only been twenty years old. Nineteen when they started dating. Not even old enough to vote, or drink, or anything.

Rae had never been so humiliated, and the cute blouses she'd bought had helped for about a week.

She flashed a smile at Paige, a pretty blonde who'd owned the boutique for a decade. Her mother had started it in Island Park in the eighties, and Paige regularly went down to New York City to keep up with the latest styles.

"So what's new?" she asked as she started browsing. "Anything Missy might like?"

"I don't sell cowgirl boots," Paige said with a laugh. "You should get Missy her favorite chocolate. Or, I know!" Her curls bounced as she smiled and accentuated her words with hand gestures. "There's that coupon book that several of the restaurants teamed up to create. Discounts on everything from coffee at The Bean to pizza to a night at the movies. I bet she and Tucker would love that."

Rae beamed at Paige. "That's a great idea." She'd known about the Island Park Business Collective, as they'd approached the rec center about including a coupon in the book. But Rae didn't have to deal with that, so she hadn't paid much attention to it. "I should get one of those for myself. I don't cook nearly as often as I should."

She fingered the cotton of a pink and white blouse. "Could I get away with wearing pink?" She lifted the flowery garment from the rack and held it up to her body.

"Everyone can get away with wearing pink." Paige plucked another top from another rack and extended it toward Rae. "And you need this."

Rae fell in love with the navy blue sweater with short sleeves and bright red hearts. She was a sucker for anything with a heart on it, and she happily took the hanger from Paige. "I'll be right back."

After she'd tried on the sweater and the blouse, and purchased both, she headed down the sidewalk again. She should be able to get a coupon book at any participating business, and she happened to be in the mood for some spaghetti and meatballs from the best Italian restaurant in town.

Okay, so La Ferrovia's was the *only* Italian restaurant in town, but only because no one could compete with their half-and-half spaghetti special. Half homemade Alfredo sauce, half house-made marinara and enough spaghetti and sausage meatballs to kill a small horse. Rae's mouth watered just thinking about it.

She passed the barber shop—now closed—and the bustling movie theater on the other side of the street before coming to La Ferrovia. She went halfway down the side of the building and entered there, where she knew the take-out counter was. She'd have to wait, but she didn't mind.

She placed her order with Matteo, the second-generation son of the founder, and asked, "And do you have those coupon books for the businesses in town?"

"Sure do." Matteo looked Italian, but he spoke without an accent, having been born and raised in Island Park just like Rae. She'd even gone out on a date or two with him. It felt like Rae had been out on a date or two with every eligible man in town.

"I need two." Rae passed over her debit card and a healthy smile for Matteo. Just like with every other man in town, there was no spark between her and Matteo. No spark between her and Zack.

There had been a spark with Damian, one that had been extinguished so rapidly that Rae still felt cold sometimes. But he'd lied. He'd lied about his age. Lied about where he'd grown up, and gone to college, and did for a living. Lied about all of it.

Matteo handed her card back and slid two coupon books across the counter. "Fifteen minutes on the spaghetti," he said, and Rae retreated to a row of chairs specifically for take-out customers.

Only moments later, the bell on the take-out entrance door rang. Zack came through it with two other guys who worked at the rec center. Rae's heart seized when they caught sight of her waiting there alone.

"Hey," Zack said in the easy way he had. He parked himself next to her. "Getting take-out?"

"Well, I'm not holding down this chair for no reason."

He laughed, the way he always did when she gave him a little attitude. "Me and the guys are loading up on lasagna and playing cards tonight. You want to come?"

No, Rae did not want to go. She wasn't one of the guys, and she hated being treated like she was. At least outside of work. At the center, she wanted her opinions to count for as much as anyone else's. But that had also been one of her and Zack's biggest problems: He didn't see a sexy, desirable woman when he looked at her. He saw "one of the guys."

"No thanks," Rae said. "I've already got plans."

He wouldn't ask what they were. He never did. "All right." Zack glanced at the coupon books. "Loading up on take-out bargains?"

"One's for Missy. It's her birthday."

"Oh, right. Gladys has been baking for days now. I should've known." He chuckled and stood when one of the guys turned toward him and gestured him toward the counter.

Rae watched him take several loaves of garlic cheese bread while the other men gathered up the lasagna pan and a large salad. He lived on the same street as Gladys Bright, who lived next door to Tucker and Missy. Gladys was known for her pies— and her willingness to share around the neighborhood.

"See ya," Zack called over his shoulder, and Rae lifted her hand in farewell. She wasn't sure why a trickle of relief spread through her. She liked Zack. She had no problem working with him, and their conversations were always easy and relaxed.

Maybe being around him socially just reminds you of why you need cute blouses to stand out at work, she thought.

But she didn't really know, couldn't really put her finger on why she liked Zack at work but wanted different treatment outside the walls of the rec center.

"Rae." Matteo set a foam container on the counter, and Rae banished her thoughts in favor of marinara and parmesan cheese.

RAE TEXTED BEN ALL THROUGH CHURCH, SEEING AS HE SAT AGAINST
the wall again, a barricade of brothers between her and him. She
didn't hear a word Pastor Gray said, and she wasn't all that sorry
about it.

I'm totally going to have to repent, she sent. *Have you heard
anything the preacher has said?*

Sure, Ben replied. *He's talking about being patient in our personal
reformation.*

How can you listen and text?

I'm a man of many talents.

Rae had to stifle a laugh then, and a warm glow cascaded over
her skin. She hadn't felt this tingle of attraction for a long time.
Damian hadn't made her laugh; he'd made her feel like jumping
on the back of his motorcycle and setting her sights on the
big city.

Ben was his complete opposite, and Rae liked that he made
her smile, made her laugh, made her feel a measure of happiness
she hadn't in a while. She tucked her phone under her leg and
made it to the end of the meeting, but by the time she got to the
back of the chapel, the Buttars brothers were long gone.

Work exploded that week, what with the final round of the
softball tournament approaching and the youth soccer practices
starting. Rae spent more time in the shed at the Sports Complex
than her office at the rec center, which suited her just fine.

She sent Ben quick texts whenever she could, but she didn't
see him until the following Saturday, when she drove the five
miles from the town to the farm. She pulled into the dirt parking
lot used by the public and climbed from her sedan.

She tucked her hands into her back pockets and drew in a
deep breath of crisp morning air, the tickle of her hair over her
shoulders increasing with the breeze. She'd forgotten how
peaceful Steeple Ridge could be. The way it held dust from ages

ago spoke of a slower pace of life, with open blue skies and wide green pastures and those perfectly white picket fences.

Rae craved a slower pace of life, especially in the summer. "Just make it until September," she muttered to herself.

"Talkin' to yourself?"

She turned to find Ben nearly at her side, a shy smile on his face and his cowboy hat pushed low over his brow.

"I used to ride here." She reached her hand halfway toward him, hoping he'd make up the rest of the distance. He did, and she sighed as his large hand engulfed hers. She may have leaned into him, she wasn't sure. He was suddenly half a step behind her, his body so close and so warm.

Her heartbeat stumbled and skipped ahead even as a smile sprang to her face. "This is nice."

"Being at the farm? Or holding my hand? Or talking to yourself?"

She giggled and said, "All of it."

He inhaled, his chest pushing into her shoulder. "So, do you want to ride?" He half-turned toward the barn and she went with him.

"I haven't been on a horse in a long time," she said, all the reasons she'd left Steeple Ridge in the first place flooding through her mind.

"Gotta start somewhere." He tugged her forward, and she went. She went, because she'd come out here to observe him give a horseback riding lesson. She went, because she'd volunteered to be his first student.

She went, because she didn't want to leave Ben's side.

9

Self-consciousness engulfed Ben with every step toward the main barn. Sure, he'd known about Rae's medals. He'd known she'd ridden a horse before. But it had suddenly become real. She swung their hands between them easily, and she didn't pull away when Missy appeared in the doorway of her office in the main barn.

"Hey, Rae," she said, her eyes easily finding their joined hands.

"Missy." Rae released Ben's hand and stepped into the other woman for a hug. "I have your birthday present in the car." She glanced at Ben. "We have time, right?"

"All day," he said, backing up until he reached the stalls behind him. He watched Missy and Rae head back into the morning sunshine, the air in the barn so suffocating. He hadn't seen Rae in eight days—the back of her head at church six days ago didn't count—and though they'd texted all week, being in her presence sent fire through his bloodstream.

His cowboy hat felt like it was squeezing his brain. So tight, so tight. He removed the hat and ran his hands through his hair. He hadn't had much practice getting control of his hormones, and he certainly didn't know how to start now.

Deep breath in. His head cleared the slightest bit. He turned toward the stall where he stood, and a horse moseyed over to him, a soft snuffle on her lips. "Hey, Brighton." The mare had a coat like a cow, all black and white and spotted.

He stroked the horse's neck, a sense of calm infusing him with the simple touch. "So you're a girl. What kinds of things do women like?" He wasn't sure why he thought Rae didn't like him. She held his hand. Initiated the contact even. She laughed at the lame things he said.

"Flowers?" he guessed anyway. "Oh, I know. Pretzels." He smiled at the horse as she closed her eyes lazily.

"Did you say pretzels?" Rae appeared at his side. She patted the horse too, absolutely no fear of the animal. At least the horseback riding lesson would go well. He hoped.

"You have a one-track mind," he said. "Always using me for my baking skills."

"What else can you make?"

"Not much," he admitted. "Are we still on for dinner tonight?"

"Yep. I bought a coupon book."

Ben frowned and studied her face as she looked at the horse. "What does that have to do with anything?"

"You know, one of those coupon books from the Business Collective?"

Ben stared at her blankly, and she nudged him with her shoulder. "You really don't get to town much, do you?"

"You thought I was lying about that?"

"What? No." She jerked away from the horse and pocketed her hands. "Should we get started?"

Surprised at the quick change in her, at the slight iciness emanating from her, he gestured down the aisle. "We need to go to the back barn."

Rae moved, and Ben joined his step to hers. "Siblings?" he asked.

"None. My dad left my mom when I was a baby."

"I'm sorry," he murmured.

"Oh, don't be," she said. "My mom is great. I don't even know where my father is." Rae tossed him a sideways smile he wanted to memorize and replay in the soft moments before he fell asleep. She jerked to a halt. "Ben, I'm sorry. That sounded so...callous. I'm sorry." She put her hand on his arm.

Ben swallowed, though her remark hadn't cut him too deeply. "My dad was great," he said. "He'd go out back and throw a football with anyone who wanted to, any time. Even when he was tired after a long day of work." He put a smile on his face, the memories of his father filled with joy. "And I got the baking skills from my mom. She—" Emotion surged up his throat, silencing his vocal chords. He held the knowledge that his mom had baked soft pretzels the day before she'd been killed close. So close.

Rae's hand tightened, and she swept into his personal space, her lips brushing his cheek. Explosions went off, snapping and popping and tingling across his skin and down into his gut. "I'm sorry."

In another life, one where Ben got to finish high school and take girls to prom, he would've known what to do. He would've swept Rae into his arms and held her tight. Kissed her, maybe.

But in this life, he just stood there and gazed into her face. So honest, so open, so sincere. "Thanks," he finally said. He cleared his throat and stepped away from her touch, the apple-y smell of her skin. Tart and sweet at the same time, the scent of her almost driving him to madness.

"So my horse is named Willow," he said as she matched his stride. "I'm going to have you ride one named Capone."

"Like Al Capone?" Rae's voice went up in pitch. "I don't know how I feel about that."

"What was your horse's name? The one you won all those

medals with?" He pushed open the back door and held it for her to walk through first.

"Sneaky."

He grinned at her, heat rising through his chest, painting his throat and face in delicious fire. "I'm going to see those medals."

"Promises, promises." She sashayed through the door and he followed, a chuckle coming from his mouth. He led her to Capone's stall and let the brown and white animal approach them.

"He's real gentle," Ben said. "He'll definitely be used in the program. So first we're going to let the horses get comfortable with us." He took her hand and lifted it to Capone's mane. "So just give him a pat."

She stroked the horse, a half-smile on her face that spoke of contentment. Ben was sure the kids in the riding lessons wouldn't be so fearless, and he'd have to figure out what to do with them if they wouldn't touch the horse.

"We'll put a bridle on him and lead him around."

"You said we could ride today." Rae flashed him a look of mild annoyance. "This isn't my first rodeo."

"Yeah, but it's been twenty years."

"Hey. Only eighteen."

Ben tried not to notice that he was barely older than that. Still, his first couple of words got stuck when he said, "We'll go slow, then."

She turned away from the horse. "I'll get the saddles."

"Right." Ben scoffed. "You don't work here. I'll get what we need." He strode away from her before she could protest, returning with the equipment she'd need to saddle Capone. "I'll meet you outside," he said before walking down a few stalls to where Willow waited for him.

He had his horse saddled and outside nibbling grass for fifteen minutes before Rae showed up with Capone in tow. He cocked his eyebrow at her. "Still want to ride today?"

"Yes," she said stubbornly, setting her mouth in a straight line. Ben only half-wished he didn't find it so sexy.

"All right. You need help getting on?"

"No." Her clipped words didn't fall on deaf ears. At least Ben could hear her frustration and knew to back down. Or rather, away, as she swung herself wildly to the side in her attempt to land in the saddle.

Somehow she did it, and Ben was sure some sort of magic had been at play. She'd practically been horizontal in the air. He shook his head, another laugh sitting at the base of his throat, and mounted his own horse.

"We can just wander through the woods," he suggested. "Yeah?"

"Sure." She held the reins in her hands the right way, so maybe she'd be fine. He started Willow at a mere walk, barely putting one hoof more than a few feet in front of the other. It made a nice atmosphere for talking, and this time, he wanted her to do most of that. He'd already gone off about his family and all the ranches where he and his brothers had worked.

"So how'd you get into recreational management?" he asked.

"I went to college in Montpelier," she said. "I started in human resources, but I got bored pretty fast. I played tennis, so I started in sports management, and eventually moved into recreational management."

Ben blinked. "So it's a real thing?"

"You just asked me how I got into it."

"I didn't know it was an actual program or a degree or anything."

"Well, it is." Her tone could've been frosty. Or she could've just been saying recreational management was a degree. Ben was exhausted trying to figure everything out. "I did work in the human resources department at the rec center for a few years before a management position became available."

"You like your work?"

"Sure," she said. "I mean, I work with about sixty-five men, and just one of me, but it's okay."

Ben didn't know how to respond. He hadn't realized she was so surrounded by males. Something he could only describe as jealousy surged up his throat. "I saw a woman there last week when I came by."

"Yeah, Meredith. She's a front desk receptionist."

"So just no women in management."

"Not really, no. At least here in Island Park."

Ben nodded though Rae wasn't looking at him. He wasn't sure why he cared who she worked with. He hadn't even known it could be a problem, but the fact that she worked with dozens of other men didn't sit right in his chest. What if she decided she liked one of them better than him?

He didn't know what to do with these types of feelings, and they pushed, pulsed against the back of his tongue. He tried swallowing, but that didn't really help. So he said, "Favorite food?" and hoped they would go away the more she talked.

By the time they circled through the woods and returned to the barn, all Ben could think about was kissing Rae. Make sure she knew he wanted to spend a lot more time with her before he unleashed her back to the rec center—and all those men—on Monday morning.

She brushed down Capone with the loving touch of someone who'd taken good care of a horse in the past. She murmured to him, and Ben found himself leaning toward her, trying to catch what she was telling the animal. He never could make out distinct words though.

"So you'll come get me in a couple of hours?" She stepped into his side, and he automatically lifted his arm and put it around her waist.

"Sure," he said. "And you're going to take us somewhere with your coupon. I mean, I'm paying, but you pick where we go."

"I was thinking...." She tilted her head back and looked up at him. He stopped walking, the moment between them stretching into something meaningful.

"Thinking what?" he managed to push out of his throat.

"Maybe you'd be okay to drive up to Burlington," she said. "There are a lot more choices for places to eat, and we could walk through their Sugar Maple Park. They have lights in all the trees in the spring."

"All right," he said stupidly, thinking he'd probably fly to Egypt with her if she wanted to go.

"You do know that Vermont is the largest producer of maple syrup, right?" Her eyes held a teasing edge.

"I did not know that."

She smiled at him, and the gesture seemed just for him. Just for him in this moment, and no one else. "They put the lights in the trees in the spring, because they tap them for the sap and they work around the clock."

"Oh." Why wouldn't his brain send words to his mouth? "Sounds fun."

She started walking again, and Ben's mind started functioning a little better without her beautiful brown eyes gazing into his.

"So four o'clock?"

Ben realized they'd made it back to her car. "Yeah, four," he said. "I'll come pick you up." He smiled and took both her hands in his, enjoying the flush that stained her cheeks a pretty pink.

She stepped back and got in the car, waving to him one final time before leaving the farm. He watched her go until he couldn't see her car anymore, almost numb to the warmth of the sun and the rustling of the breeze.

He turned back to the farmhouse and saw all three of his brothers sitting on top of the picnic table, watching him. They all wore smiles the size of Jupiter, and Ben groaned as he walked in their direction.

"Are you going out with her then?" Darren asked.

"Have you kissed her yet?" Logan wanted to know.

"That doesn't look like goin' slow," Sam said.

Ben climbed on the picnic table with them, for the first time feeling somewhat like their equal instead of the lost, little brother. "Dinner tonight," he said. "In Burlington, where apparently they have a big park full of sugar maple trees with lights in them."

"Sounds romantic," Sam said.

Ben's throat tightened. "Shoot. It does." He glanced down the row of brothers. "What does that mean?"

Logan started laughing, and Darren said, "It means you better kiss her under all those mapley lights."

"Not a good idea," Sam muttered.

"It's a great idea," Darren argued. "Did you just see them? All he had to do was lean down and she'd have let him kiss her."

Ben lost the ability to swallow. He could've kissed Rae just now? Why hadn't he done that? Did she want him to?

"Really?" he asked.

Logan snorted and leaned around Sam. "Ben, come *on*. Do you not see the way she looks at you?"

Confusion puckered his brow. "I see her...look at me," he said as if the words didn't go in that order.

"It's too soon to kiss her," Sam said with authority in his voice.

"Oh, please," Logan said. "Like you didn't kiss Kacie on the first date."

Sam's face reddened the slightest bit. "Her name was Laci."

"My point is, it's never too soon to kiss a woman," Logan said. "Especially one like Rae."

"What does that mean?" Ben asked, still a little surprised Sam had kissed a woman the very first time they'd gone out.

Logan finally sobered. "It means, Benny-Boy, that she's beautiful and available and someone else is gonna snatch her up if you don't make her yours."

Ben's jaw clenched. The idea of Rae going out with someone else, holding someone else's hand, possibly kissing another man, sent a different kind of fire through his system. Not a good fire. A raging, hissing, forest fire.

"A woman is not a possession," Sam said.

Ben met his oldest brother's eye. "I like her," he said simply, hoping Sam would understand and appreciating that he could talk to his brothers like this.

"She knows that already."

"I don't want her to go out with someone else."

"She isn't going to, whether you kiss her tonight or not." Sam's eyes softened, and Ben saw the kindness of his father shining within their depths. "Go slow, Ben. For you as much for her."

Logan hopped down from the table. "Your funeral, brother." Darren went with him into the farmhouse, leaving Ben to contemplate his options with a silent Sam.

He wanted to kiss Rae, badly. But he also had no idea how to even get his lips close to hers. She'd kissed his cheek, and she seemed well-practiced at showing affection to a man. *Of course she is*, Ben thought. *She's ten years older than you and hasn't spent the last decade wandering from ranch to ranch.*

"Be careful," Sam said as he stepped to the ground. "And go shower. A woman like Rae expects her date to smell like anything but horses." He grinned and danced away before Ben could roll his eyes. Of course he was going to shower. But honestly, Rae had been at home on top of horse. She'd been with him for a couple of hours, all horsey-smelling.

But tonight—he had a good feeling about tonight, and Sam was definitely right. Ben needed to shower before his date, especially if he hoped for a kiss by the end of the evening.

10

R ae arrived back at her house on a high. A cloud, really.
At least until she saw the silver truck sitting in her
driveway.

"Zack," she muttered under her breath as she parked along-
side him. He got out of his truck as she rounded the front of it.
"What's going on?"

"There's been a snafu at the Sports Complex."

Rae shook her head. "No. I planned everything perfectly. No
snafus possible."

"You double-booked field five. There's supposed to be two
games on it at six o'clock tonight." He pulled a bulging folder
from his truck. "We've got to figure out what to do with those two
teams, and we have an hour to do it."

She sighed like he was her mother and wouldn't let her leave
the house wearing so much makeup. "Come on in, I guess." She
practically stomped toward the front door, where her army of
animals waited in their soldier-straight lines to greet her.

She bent down and lavished attention on Beauty and then
Peaches while Zack side-stepped all the furry friends. Another

reason they would never have worked out. She didn't understand people who didn't like pets.

Zack dropped the folder on her kitchen table, creating a loud thunking noise that brought her away from her dogs. She cast him an annoyed glance and checked the time. If fixing the schedule really took an hour, she'd have thirty minutes to get ready for her dinner date in the city.

Not enough time.

She exhaled and sat at the table. "I have thirty minutes, tops." She pulled the folder toward her and opened it.

"Oh yeah?" Zack asked. "Big night tonight?"

She pressed her lips together and spread out the few papers on the top. One listed the names of the teams in the finals of the softball tournament. Another held the bracket, and she focused on that one.

It took several seconds, and Zack pointing to field five, before Rae found the mistake. She got up and retrieved a pencil from her junk drawer in the kitchen. "All right. Let's just start again."

The bracket didn't take that long to do. She could finish this and get him out of here in a half an hour, no problem.

Forty-five minutes later, she tossed the pencil onto the table-top. "How did we let too many teams register for the tournament?"

Zack shrugged, seemingly unconcerned about the blunder. "What else can we do?"

"Have those two teams play at the elementary school? It's just across the street."

"We'd need a field crew to prep everything. I'd need to call Glen and get permission to use the grounds."

That sounded like a lot of work, not to mention a change in location usually upset coaches and parents, even if it was just across the street. "We could extend the tournament by an hour," she said. "Have the last game at ten-thirty instead of nine-thirty." The thought of asking Burke to work another hour, then stay well past midnight to make sure everything got cleaned up, made her head pound.

Zack studied the bracket in front of him. "I think that's the only solution."

"I'll go over and help Burke get cleaned up." Rae stood and took her phone with her. "Are we done?"

"I'll just finish up the bracket and get it out to Burke and our team leaders," he said. "You go do what you need to do."

She walked down the hall toward her bedroom and bathroom, her thumbs flying over her phone. *I'm so sorry, Burke. I'll be there by eleven to help with take-down.* She hit send, expecting several questions since she hadn't explained anything—Zack would do that—and silenced her phone.

She just wanted an hour of peace and quiet. Of pampering herself and primping to perfection for Ben. She set her phone on its charger and turned on the smart radio wired through her ceiling with the simple command of, "House, play the playlist Rae, Adele."

Sighing and relaxing, she stepped into the hot water of the shower, letting the stress of the last hour wash down the drain. She washed and dried and dressed and brushed. She curled eyelashes and hair, sang along to her favorite soul songs, and emerged from her bedroom with three minutes to spare.

She paused as she heard two male voices conversing in the living room.

Two male voices?

And it wasn't exactly conversing, but more like arguing.

She practically flew down the hall despite the heels she'd chosen to go with her skinny jeans and that form-filling, short-sleeved sweater with hearts.

Her heart dropped to her peep-toes and rebounded to the top of her skull—painfully—when she found Ben standing near the front door, his arms folded across his broad chest, squared off with Zack, who leaned against the back of the couch, clear aggression in his stance.

"Guys?" she asked, still fiddling with the back of her earring.

"Hey, Rae," Zack said, seemingly without a care in the world. He didn't look at her though, and she wondered why in the world he hadn't left a long time ago.

"What's going on?" she asked. "Is there another problem with the schedule?" She made sure she practically yelled the last question so Ben would know Zack was here on a work-related issue. Nothing more.

"No, schedule is fine. Explained everything to everyone."

"Perfect," Rae said with a false note of *everything's-settled-here* in her tone. "So you're leaving now? Because we are."

"I don't know," Ben said.

Rae's heart did that weird free fall and spring back thing again. "You don't know what?"

"I'm leaving," Zack said, jangling his keys. He edged past Ben, who barely gave him room to exit, and cast a final glance at Rae. A final glance at Rae that she couldn't interpret. He didn't look happy, but he didn't look unhappy either. Then he was gone.

The door closed behind him, and the air felt twice as thick as she tried to breathe it in. "Sorry I'm a few minutes late," she said, though she wasn't. He'd been a few minutes early.

"Why did Zack McCoy answer your door?" He didn't budge from his position in front of the door. He could blend in with her dogs seamlessly.

"We had a scheduling problem with the tournament tonight. I thought he'd be long-gone by now." Why he hadn't left plagued her.

"So I wouldn't find out."

"Find out what?" Rae's patience ran dry in under two seconds. "There's nothing to find out about. He's my boss. I make a mistake on something work-related, and we worked together to fix it.

That's all." She took a few daring steps toward him. "We're still going to dinner, right?"

She drank in the tall, toned frame of him. The spectacular way he wore blue jeans. The sexy and sophisticated—and patriotic—red, white, and blue-striped polo. And that cowboy hat. She sucked in a breath and held it. She *really* liked his black cowboy hat.

She tripped her fingertips up his chest, fiddling with the top button on his polo, one he'd left undone. "I'm starving."

Starving for what, she couldn't exactly say. But it had been a very long time since she'd kissed a man, and Ben's lips looked perfectly kissable. Perfectly sized to capture hers and kiss her like he meant it.

Desire dove through her and she added a smile to her ensemble. "You look nice tonight," she said.

Ben finally thawed, his demeanor falling with his shoulders. "I'll admit I'm new at this dating thing," he said. "But I didn't like showing up at your house when there was another man here."

Rae blinked at him, realizing that he was jealous. And he didn't wear it all that well. She tipped her head back and laughed. And laughed.

11

Ben did not like the way Rae laughed at his confession. He didn't like it at all.

He did like the tingle of her fingertips against his chest. He did like the feel of her next to him. He did like the fruity scent of her perfume, and the hearts on her sweater, and the curve of her hips.

He reached out and put his hand on her waist, effectively silencing her. At least he seemed to affect her as strongly as she affected him. "What's so funny?" he asked.

She blinked, the passion and desire he'd seen in her eyes for a microsecond disappearing. "You being jealous of Zack. Trust me when I say there's nothing there to be jealous of."

"No?" Ben hated the accusation in his tone. "Word around the farm is that you two used to date."

"Word around the farm?"

"Sam told me."

"Used to," Rae said. "We're friends now. He's my boss. Nothing more."

Ben tried to detect any insincerity in her tone, her expression.

He couldn't find any. "I guess I'll have to trust you. I have no other way of knowing."

She cocked her head and studied him, a blip of hurt passing through her eyes. He didn't entirely hate the way she watched him, but the longer she looked, the more uncomfortable he became. He finally looked away, his eyes landing on that blasted cat that had escaped last week.

"Ben," she said, and he adored the way his name sounded against her tongue.

He looked back at her, bringing his other hand to her waist and pulling her a twitch closer. "I don't like how I feel," he murmured. "I'm all...twisted up. I don't—I—" He swallowed, hoping Rae would say something to save him. She didn't.

"I like you," he finally finished. Sam's words echoed in his head. *Go slow. It's too soon to kiss her. Go slow. Too soon. Too soon.*

She relaxed in his arms, smiling up at him with the radiance of a star. "I like you too, Ben."

He allowed himself a smile too. "So where did you want to go for dinner?" He stepped sideways and opened her front door. "Oh, and can we take your car? Sam dropped me off and left."

"Sam dropped you off?"

Foolishness tripped through him. He felt like he'd been driven over by his father. "We only have the one truck, and they need it tonight. I texted you about it."

She glanced down at her phone, where a blue light flashed furiously. "I can drive," she said. "Let me grab my keys."

"I'll drive," he said. "If you want."

"Do you know where we're going?" She danced away from him, a tease and a sparkle about her.

"No, ma'am."

She pulled open a drawer and extracted a set of keys. "Then I'll drive." Rae didn't come back toward him but went through the door off the kitchen and into her garage.

Ben followed her, nerves and jealousy and joy all swirling

together into a perfect storm inside his chest. He paused while still inside the house and took a deep breath. Told himself to calm down. He'd been out on a date before.

Just not for a long, long time.

And certainly not with someone as beautiful and as interesting as Rae.

"You coming?" she called, and Ben stopped giving himself a mental pep talk and joined her in the garage.

Rae navigated them north with the question of, "Do you like sushi?"

Ben made a face before he could stop himself.

Rae laughed. "All right. I'm still in my search for someone in Island Park that likes it."

"So this is a common question you ask people?"

"Not really, no." She flashed a quick smile in his direction. "I keep trying to get my mom to eat it. She refuses. I think she's actually a vegetarian."

"Fish is definitely out then." Ben watched as some of the prettiest country went by beyond his window. "Especially *raw* fish."

"Have you ever tried it?"

"No," he said.

"Might be good."

"That's what Sam said about vegemite," Ben said. "And that was disgusting."

Rae tipped her head back and laughed, filling the car with delight. Ben really liked making her laugh.

"What have you tried that you didn't like?" he asked.

"Mushrooms," she said immediately. "Tomatoes. Mandarin oranges."

"So you're definitely not a vegetarian." He kicked a smile in her direction, a chuckle vibrating in his chest.

"Definitely not. I grew up in rural Vermont. We eat beef."

Ben reached across the console and collected her hand in his.

"So where are you taking me for dinner? And isn't it kind of early for dinner?"

"We can eat now, and then get dessert later."

"Ice cream?"

"Is that your favorite dessert?"

"Absolutely."

"Noted."

Ben's muscles twitched. Noted? What did that mean? Should he be taking notes of her likes and dislikes too?

Of course you should, he told himself. *Mushrooms, tomatoes, mandarin oranges.*

"So if I wanted to bring you your favorite dessert, what would that be?" he asked.

"Salted caramel smothered in milk chocolate." She ducked her chin toward him. "*Milk.* Chocolate. Not dark. That's a common misconception."

"What is?"

"That dark chocolate is better than milk chocolate." She looked at him so long, he thought she'd drive right off the road.

"Noted," he said, which caused her to laugh again.

———

SHE TOOK HIM TO A GERMAN RESTAURANT, WHICH SERVED THINGS like pork schnitzel with mushroom cream sauce—which Rae did not order—and a mixed sausage plate with potatoes.

The whole menu seemed to be taken up with various cuts of pork and beef, along with potatoes in every variation possible. Ben thought it would've been nice to have been born in Germany.

He and Rae shared a Gypsy Plate, which included pork chops, shishkabobs, beef sausages, Hungarian rice, fried potatoes, and sauerkraut.

"Oh, and spatzle," Rae told the waiter. He nodded and walked away, leaving Rae to beam at Ben. "It's German pasta."

"And we won't have nearly enough food with all those sausages and stuff." Ben lifted his glass of water to his lips and drank. "Did you see they had an entire page of German sausage meals?"

"They're good too," Rae said.

"You come here a lot?"

"I've been up here several times, yes." She settled her arms on the table and clamped her lips shut.

The green-eyed monster reared inside Ben's soul. He wondered how many other dates had brought her to this restaurant, and it was only a miracle that he didn't ask. Instead he said, "Why did you stop riding when you were seventeen?"

She blinked, further shuttering her feelings. "Personal reasons."

Obviously. Ben studied her, trying to decide if he could push her a little further. She sighed and leaned back in her chair, moving her hands to her lap. "Personal reasons I might learn one day?"

Rae gave him a closed-mouth smile, and he didn't like it nearly as much as the one she usually graced him with. "I suppose."

He leaned forward. "Do you have a lot of secrets?"

She inched toward him too. "Wouldn't you like to know?" Her eyes glittered like diamonds, and Ben wanted to kiss her so badly he almost lunged across the table and planted one on her right there.

"Bread," the waiter said, placing a plate between them. Ben leaned back as their drinks followed, and by the time the waiter said their food would be right out, the moment between him and Rae had fled.

"I would like to know," Ben said anyway. "But you can tell me whenever you want."

"What about you?" Rae asked as she reached for her iced tea. "Do you have a lot of secrets?"

Ben chuckled and shook his head. "I'm like an open book. You already know my parents passed away. And that I've worked on a dozen farms and ranches. And that I like you."

"And that sums up your life?"

"Pretty much, yeah." Ben's inadequacies surged. Working ranches and missing his parents *did* sum up his life. How boring was that?

"Which brother do you like the most?" Rae asked.

"Easy." Ben grinned. "Sam."

"Hmm." Rae tilted her chin toward the table and looked up at him flirtatiously from under her eyelashes. "I always thought Logan was the most handsome."

Ice speared right through Ben's chest. His mouth worked itself open and then closed. Open and closed.

Rae's glorious laughter knocked him out of his stupor. "I was joking," Rae said. "Sam's definitely the best looking." She punctuated the sentence with another laugh, this time with Ben joining in.

———

TWO HOURS LATER, AND FULLY SATIATED WITH PORK, POTATOES, AND pasta, Ben tucked Rae into his side and walked down the path toward the grove of sugar maples. The park did seem magical at dusk, and when the lights winked to life in the trees, a sense of wonder engulfed Ben.

"Feels like Christmas," he murmured.

"I love this park."

"You must come here often too."

"My mom brought me every spring when I was little."

Embarrassment mixed with his lingering jealousy, creating a bad taste in Ben's mouth. He didn't know what to say, so he didn't say anything. He enjoyed every step through the maze of trees, loved listening to Rae speak about the maple sap spigots, basked in the warmth of the lanterns in the leaves until full dark had settled over the sugar maples.

"We better get going," Rae said. "I have to go to the Sports Complex and help take down."

"You have to go to work tonight?"

"Yeah, I overbooked the ball fields, so we had to push back one of the games. If I go help Burke, my foreman, we'll both be able to get out of there sooner."

"I can come." Ben didn't want to drop her off with another man.

She unlocked the car and paused to look at him. "I do have to drive you home...."

"And you said we'd get ice cream."

A smile burst onto her face. "I said we'd get a dessert."

"And I said ice cream, and you said sure."

She laughed and pushed his chest. "I don't remember it that way."

He stumbled back like she really had the strength to push him several feet. "But we can get ice cream, right?"

"There's a Ben & Jerry's around here somewhere."

"Map it," he said. "I love their peanut butter passion." Ben started around the car.

"Really?"

He paused. "Don't tell me you don't like peanut butter."

She shrugged one shoulder, the movement sexy and strong. "It's okay. I like the raspberry cheesecake."

Ben made a face. "Fruit should not be eaten with cake. Or ice cream." He gave a fake shudder and detoured back toward Rae. "I'll drive."

"Oh, you will, huh?" She held the keys out to her side, like he wouldn't be able to get them there, a purely delighted smile on her face.

He swiped them from her with one long arm, and swept the

other around her waist, drawing her close to his body. "I think I can get us back from here."

She relaxed into him, putting both her hands on his shoulders. "What about the ice cream?"

"Maybe you can navigate me?" He dipped his head, and she froze in his arms. He thought about kissing her, and he knew she was thinking about kissing him, what with the way her eyes focused on his mouth.

At least she'd entertained the idea. Maybe even wanted to kiss him.

Too soon.

He stepped back and clicked the unlock button on her key fob. "So let's go. I'll even buy you that fruity ice cream."

————

BEN BATHED BAYS AND SORRELS AND ROANS. HE FIXED FENCES AND mended the railing on the front porch at the farmhouse. He kept the lawn trimmed and took Willow for long rides through the woods. He texted Rae whenever he thought of something she might want to know about, or that she might laugh at, or just when he wanted to feel closer to her.

It didn't seem like such a hard thing to drive five miles into town, but Ben couldn't seem to carve out the time to do it. Rae couldn't either, but at least she had a good reason. Her work occupied twelve hours of her day. Ben simply didn't have his own car, and he didn't want to ask Sam to borrow the truck when he had no other reason than to go see Rae.

So he texted. And she texted back.

At the end of the week, Ben summoned all his bravery and messaged her with, *Will you sit by me at church?*

What? All the way against the wall with your brothers beside us?

He grinned at her quick response, her quick wit. *No, just me and you. Wherever you want to sit.*

Can you even do that?

Why wouldn't I be able to do that?

I've never seen the Buttars brothers sit anywhere but on the third bench from the back on the right side.

He chuckled. Sam was a creature of habit if there ever was one. *I'm about to break the mold.*

Don't strain yourself.

A full-blown laugh burst from Ben's mouth and filled the sky above him. Hope and happiness filled all the hollowness inside him. Hollowness he'd known was there and thought he'd just have to live with for the rest of his life. Intellectually, he knew people experienced a measure of happiness he didn't know. He'd seen it in his parents, especially when he looked at the photos of them in the albums he'd brought with him from the house in Wyoming.

He just hadn't known how it would feel. Like his mother was there to bake him soft pretzels, smile at him from across the kitchen counter, scoot the ketchup bottle a little closer so he could dip his carbs in his favorite condiment.

"What are you laughin' at?" Sam paused on his way out of the farmhouse, his arms full of freshly laundered horse blankets.

Ben shoved his phone in his back pocket. "Nothing."

"Good. Come do *nothing* in the barn with me."

"I've finished all my chores." Ben didn't even flinch toward getting off the picnic table. "I was going to check the sprinkling system again. It didn't come on this morning."

Sam looked him up and down. Once, twice. "All right then."

Ben smiled at his brother until Sam strode away, his cowboy boots kicking up dust as he went. The heat of the almost-summer day beat down on the farm, and Ben reveled in the slow pace of his life, the way he could sit here and look at the puffy clouds in the sky, breathe in the fresh air, and let his mind wander down roads it hadn't traveled before.

Rambo, the Australian shepherd that Logan had picked up in

a grocery store parking lot eight years ago, came trotting around the side of the farmhouse. He panted as he collapsed in the shade beside the picnic table. "Hey, boy."

The dog barely looked at him, but Rambo had never liked Ben all that much. At the most, Rambo tolerated everyone except Logan, and only Ben still tried to make the dog like him, which was why he got down and went into the kitchen to get a big bowl of cold water for Rambo.

He returned to the back yard and set the bowl by the dog, who got up and started lapping at the water. Ben watched him with a smile on his face, especially when his phone buzzed with an incoming text.

It wasn't from Rae, but Missy. *Will Rae be coming to dinner on Sunday?*

Ben hadn't thought of that. *I don't know.*

You should ask her.

I should?

His phone rang, Missy's face coming up on the screen. "Hey," Ben answered.

"Ben, are you dating Rae or not?"

"I...guess?"

Missy half-sighed and half-laughed. Ben wasn't sure which annoyed him more. "How can you not know?"

"How would I know?" he asked. "I haven't kissed her. We've gone to dinner once. We text during the week." He swallowed and watched Rambo flop onto his side and start snoozing. "Is that dating?"

Missy said, "Hmm," and Ben waited for something more.

When she said nothing, he asked, "How did you know when you were dating Tucker?"

"About the time he took me to buy feed with him."

"That doesn't sound very romantic."

Missy laughed. "Tucker didn't know a whole lot about farming or horses when he came to Steeple Ridge. I did have to

tell him that doing work-related things didn't count as dating."
She paused and then asked, "You haven't done that, have
you Ben?"

"Well, Rae and I were working on the horseback riding
lessons together. Does that count?"

"I don't think so," Missy said. "Especially because we're not
going to do the horseback riding lessons anymore."

Ben perked up at that bit of information. "We're not?"

"No." Missy exhaled in a long hiss. "Rae doesn't have time to
really think about it, and we've already got our summer camps
going. Maybe another time."

Ben could hear an undercurrent of frustration in his friend's
voice. "The farm is plenty busy, Missy."

"I know."

"What's with the riding lessons then?"

"I don't know. I just—I loved coming out to Steeple Ridge for
horseback riding lessons when I was a little girl. Rae did too. I
just thought—I don't know. I thought it would be a good thing."

"Why did Rae stop riding?" he asked.

"Something with her dad," Missy said. "Anyway, Ben, invite
Rae to dinner on Sunday. She'll like it."

Ben agreed and hung up with Missy, his mind churning over
what she'd said about Rae's father. Rae had said that her dad had
left when she was a baby. Had said she didn't know where her
dad was now.

And she probably didn't. Ben wouldn't allow himself to
assume the worst until he knew the whole story. He wasn't sure if
he should be excited to learn as much as he could about Rae, or if
the strength of his feelings should terrify him.

No matter what, he wanted to know all the things about Rae.
The good things. The bad ones. The ones where she earned
medals. And if Missy thought she'd like dinner at the farm, then
Ben would invite Rae to dinner at the farm.

12

Rae floated through her weekend until she arrived at church. The sight of tall, tanned Ben Buttars leaning against the brown-brick church made wings erupt in her stomach. She skipped over to him and said, "Hey, there, handsome."

A smile spread his lips, real slow, like he was trying to savor it. He slid his eyes down the length of her body. "Don't you look nice?"

She brushed her hands over her navy blue pencil skirt, her frilly yellow polka dot blouse the perfect complement to it. "This old thing?"

"That is brand new," he said.

"How would a cowboy like you know that?"

"My mom had four boys," he said, pushing himself into a standing position and offering her his arm. "She taught us how to do laundry, and which detergents to use to keep colors bright." He glanced at her blouse again, and Ben possessed the penetrating gaze of a man who could somehow see right through everything. Her heart tripped and a ripple of fire trailed down her spine to her toes. "And that blouse looks like it's never been washed."

"Doesn't mean it's new."

They entered the church, and Ben glanced to the bench where his brother sat. "But it is new." He met her eye. "Right?"

"Fine." She swatted his bicep. "I bought it yesterday."

He grinned at her and swept his gaze across the chapel. "Where are we sitting?"

"How about on that pew right there?" She started down the left aisle, Ben a half-step behind her. She reached the row and slid onto it, a family down on the other end. Ben sat beside her, easily lifting his arm and settling it over her shoulders.

She crossed her legs and leaned her body into his chest. It felt nice to be sitting next to him, absorbing his warmth, enjoying his company. She'd been sitting by her mother at church since Damian had left town. Eating Sunday dinner with her mother.

Rae had never been so excited to tell her mom that she would be sitting with someone else at church. That had led to a lot of questions, but Rae hadn't minded. She'd never minded talking about her boyfriends.

There was that blasted B-word again. She'd been thinking it a lot lately—ever since Ben had asked her to church and then out to the farm for Sunday dinner. He claimed Missy cooked every weekend, and while Rae hadn't known Missy could do more than stick a pizza in the oven, she wanted to be back at Steeple Ridge. Back with Ben.

The choir started singing, a rousing number that made Rae's heart swell with joy and love. She was reminded of why she came to church, even when she worked ninety-hour weeks and would like to stay home and sleep. Even when she'd just endured an embarrassing breakup and didn't want to see her friends. Or anyone.

She'd have to tell Ben about Damian soon enough. Sooner rather than later, she knew. But for now, she just rested her head against his strong shoulder and listened to the preacher talk about being humble and meek. As he spoke, he painted the picture of Ben. Someone who didn't know how wonderful they were. Someone who thought about others and put them first. Someone the exact opposite of every other man Rae had ever dated.

As she sat next to him on that pew, Rae let herself fall a little farther. Fall where, she wasn't sure, but she knew she liked Ben a whole lot.

The rest of the sermon passed in what felt like seconds. The choir sang again, jolting Rae from her thoughts. She stood with Ben and filed out of the church, her hand in his. Everyone saw. Every woman in town now knew there was one less available Buttars brother in town. Rae kept her head down and her smile to herself, at least until she made it to the parking lot and handed Ben her keys.

"You want to change first?" he asked. "We're low-key at the farm. And we can ride this afternoon. Missy doesn't bring dinner until five." He shuffled his feet and wouldn't look directly at her.

"What?" she asked.

"Nothing."

"Ben."

His shoulders sagged. "There's a lot of hours between now and dinner."

Understanding descended on Rae. "You don't think we can fill a few hours?"

"I—"

"Because we can," Rae said. "I have a bunch of jokes from junior high I could tell, and maybe we could give Capone a bath after we ride through the forest for a while." She smiled, prepared to go on if he continued to stand there like a statue.

She opened her mouth but he said, "You'll spoil that horse."

"Oh, please." She waited for him to open the passenger-side door for her. "I'm not the one cooing to Willow every chance I get." She raised her eyebrows to make her point, then slid into the car.

Ben moved around the front of the car and got in behind the wheel. "First, I do not *coo* at my horse."

"You do too!" She laughed at the jumping muscle in his jaw, enjoying his frustration a little too much. "You don't even realize how high your voice pitches up." She giggled and reached over, taking the brim of his cowboy hat in her fingers.

He swung his gaze to her in slow motion, and she removed the hat from his head. She stared at it, unsure of what she was doing and why. She looked up, right into Ben's light brown eyes, and got stuck. Caught in the heat of his gaze.

"You have nice hair," she murmured.

Several seconds passed with this electric charge between them. "I want to kiss you," he said, his voice low and hoarse and hardly his own.

"Do it, then."

He leaned forward, setting Rae's pulse into a frenzy. Her eyes drifted halfway closed, only to be snapped open by the rapid beating of fists on the window behind Ben.

He yelped and twisted to look behind him. "Stupid," he muttered as he rolled down the window. "Logan! Darren!"

Laughter filtered back to Rae, and she joined her voice to theirs. Ben did not even crack a smile.

He gripped the steering wheel and said, "My brothers are idiots."

"Don't worry, Ben," she said. "There's a lot of hours between now and dinner."

He looked at her, pure terror on his face. She smiled and giggled as she handed his cowboy hat back to him. He mashed it low over his eyes, muttered something about why none of the brothers were married, and put the car in reverse as a ruddy flush crawled from under the collar of his white shirt.

Rae rolled down the window and let the wind blow through

her hair. It would ruin all the curls she'd worked to put in that morning, but she didn't care. Ben pulled into her driveway and flexed his fingers on the wheel. "I'll wait out here," he said.

"You can come in," she said. "My bedroom door locks."

"I'll wait."

Rae wasn't sure why he was so tight, and her joy dropped a notch. "Ben, it's no big deal. It's not like I've never had the brothers of one of my boyfriends interrupt us."

That was the absolute wrong thing to say, and she sucked in a breath as Ben trained his dangerous, storming eyes on her. He said nothing, but then again, he didn't need to.

"Be right back," she choked out and escaped from her own car. She set the house music on rock and loud, the way she had when Ben had shown up at her house unannounced. That morning seemed like it had happened months ago, but it had only been a few weeks.

She kicked off her heels and ran her fingers through her hair, belting out the lyrics to one of her childhood favorites as she moved down the hall. The walls vibrated as she changed into a pair of khaki shorts and a green and white striped V-neck. She slipped on a sensible pair of running shoes and pulled her hair into a ponytail. When she retraced her steps down the hall, she found Ben loitering in her kitchen, a bottle of water from her fridge in his hand.

She commanded the house to stop playing, and said, "You came in."

"So you just say 'House, do this,' and it does it?" He glanced up to the ceiling like there would be minions there, waiting to fulfill his every wish.

"Some things," she said. "I mean, it can't make toast or anything."

His lips twitched. "Because that would be ridiculous."

The tension beneath her breastbone lessened. "Obviously."

She moved next to him. "House, set the security system." She found herself looking up too.

"Security system armed," the speakers said in a robotic female voice. Rae beamed up at Ben. "Now you can't leave."

"Is that right?" He inched a bit closer to her.

Rae retreated. "Oh, we're not kissing here." She shook her head. "Uh uh. Not happening."

Confusion crossed Ben's expression, along with a healthy dose of humiliation. "Why not?"

"I don't want my first kiss with you to happen in my kitchen." She folded her arms and leaned against the counter behind her, gazing evenly at the man she very much wanted to kiss. Just not here.

"Where would you like it to happen?" He stalked one step closer.

"Not here."

"Why not?"

"A kitchen is not romantic."

He took another step.

"Ben," she warned.

"Rae." He closed the distance between them and placed his hands on the counter on both sides of her hips. He bent over her, the edge of his cowboy hat bumping against her forehead.

Her heart hammered against her ribcage, and she swallowed down her emotions. She wanted to kiss him, very badly. Kitchen or no kitchen.

"My brothers aren't here. They'll be everywhere at the farm."

"It's my kitchen." Her voice sounded breathy and weak.

"So you can think about kissing me every morning when you make coffee." He traced his lips down the side of her face, pausing on the edge of her jaw.

Her muscles trembled, and her resolve crumbled. She reached up and swept the cowboy hat off his head, pushing her fingers through his hair.

A smile stole across his face as he trailed a kiss across her throat.

"You're maddening," she whispered.

"So are you," he murmured just before touching his lips to hers. Sparks exploded in her mouth, and she received his kiss with excitement and eagerness. Ben explored gently, gingerly, for a few moments before truly kissing her.

And Rae had been right. He had a mouth that could kiss her like he meant it.

13

Ben had never kissed a woman the way he kissed Rae. He'd only kissed one other girl and she was nowhere near Rae's caliber. And he'd never been kissed back with quite so much passion. She ran her fingers down the back of his neck, eliciting a shiver from him, and kept on kissing him.

He wasn't sure how to stop, or when. He knew she tasted like sugar, something so addicting he couldn't give her up now even if he'd wanted to.

And he certainly didn't want to.

The connection between them eventually lapsed, and Ben kept his eyes closed as Rae tucked herself into his chest. He held her, enjoying that as much as kissing her. Well, maybe not *quite* as much. A feeling of comfort and peace flowed through him, and he thought life couldn't get any better than standing in her kitchen after a kiss.

A cat mewed, and Rae moved out of his embrace. "Hey, Cherry-Pop." She crouched in front of the cat and gave him a quick pat. "Let's get you guys some food and water." She went around the counter and bent to retrieve two bowls from the floor near the kitchen table.

"I'll help," he said, collecting two more bowls. "These must be for the dogs." He'd patted the white one, but she hadn't mentioned any names. "You have two, right?"

"Beauty and Peaches." She gestured to where a fluffy white thing sat next to a little black dog

"Beauty and Peaches," he repeated, joining her back at the kitchen sink. "How long have you had them?"

"I've had Beauty since she was a puppy, but Peaches I just got over Thanksgiving. See, I have this friend, the veterinarian? Layla —who keeps bringing all these strays to dinner when we get together. She knows I'm a huge sucker for puppy dog eyes."

Ben chuckled along with her. "Is that how you got the declawed, half-deaf cat?"

"You guessed it." She glanced down at her feet. "But I like Ralph. He's a nice cat. It's that gray one you need to watch out for."

"Cherry-Pop? He seems nice."

"He has a weight problem." She opened a cupboard in the corner and scooped a cupful of food into the bowl. "And I just keep feeding him. It's weight-control cat food, I swear."

Ben lifted one hand as if acquiescing. "Not judging you or your overweight cat." He gave her a quick smile. "We have a dog."

"Just one?"

"It's really Logan's. He's never liked me much."

"You should get one of your own."

"I like my horse just fine." He filled the water bowl and set the other one on the counter. Rae put food in it. They worked together to get the animals fed, and Ben found that he liked the mundane things it took to live when he was with Rae. It didn't matter if they went to a fancy place for dinner, or walked through a magical grove of sugar maples, or fed and watered pets on a Sunday near lunchtime.

"Thanks," she said. "Should we go?"

"Just one more thing," he said, pulling her to him for another kiss.

———

THEY DIDN'T GO STRAIGHT OUT TO STEEPLE RIDGE. RAE DIRECTED him around town, giving him a driving tour of the place. He'd lived at Steeple Ridge for nine months, but he barely knew where the grocery store was.

Rae showed him her mother's house, the elementary school where she'd gone, the historic water tower. She told him stories about the Pizza Palace, and the bowling alley, and the downtown park.

"And this is where I spend a lot of my time in the summer," Rae said as he pulled into the massive parking lot at the Sports Complex. It looked bigger when it was empty, as it was today.

"I know," Ben said. "I came to help you clean up last week, remember?" He parked at the curb near the bathrooms.

"Oh, that's right." She gave him a smile and got out of the car. "Should we walk?"

Ben didn't much care to walk around the Sports Complex, but he'd do whatever Rae wanted. He took her hand as they started on the asphalt path. "It's getting hot," he said. "Not as hot as some of the ranches I worked on in Nevada or Utah. But hot."

They approached a tree and a swelling buzz met Ben's ears. He froze.

Rae glanced over at him. "What?"

"Are those bees?" He swallowed. "I'm allergic to bees."

"Like allergic, allergic?"

"Like if I get stung, you'll need to call nine-one-one."

"Do you have an epi-pen?"

"At the farm." He turned around and headed back toward the car.

Rae caught up to him. Said, "You're cute."

"Is *cute* a compliment?"

"I like that you're allergic to bees."

"Oh yeah?"

"Yeah." She laced her arm through his and didn't give any further explanation. Ben wasn't sure why his allergies would be appealing to her, but he didn't question it. He simply wanted to get out to Steeple Ridge, get saddled up, and take her out to the clearing to kiss her again.

He didn't make it quite that far. Out to the farm, yes. Into the barn, sure. But he couldn't resist pressing her against the door of a stall and kissing her until he couldn't breathe. It wasn't until Willow nickered to him from down the aisle that he pulled back.

"She's jealous," Rae said, holding herself in place next to him, her breath mixing with his as she tried to catch it. "Should we go ride?"

"Why'd you stop riding?" he asked. Missy had mentioned something about her father, and Ben wasn't sure why he couldn't let it go.

A blip of fear pulsed through her eyes. "I was a stupid kid."

"You still love horses," he said, moving down the row and opening Willow's gate. "That much is obvious. I can only imagine you showing a horse." He threw her a grin before walking into the horse's stall.

She sighed and leaned against the stall wall. "My dad came back to town when I was seventeen. He claimed he wanted to make things right with my mother. Wanted to get to know me." She rolled her eyes, and Ben stroked his horse's mane while he watched and waited for her to continue.

"I was angry. He hadn't even sent me a birthday card once. So when my mom acted like he could just step back into her life— and thus mine—I...acted out."

"You quit riding."

"He said I was a natural. I never rode again." Sadness and

frustration filled her face, along with a sense of determination Ben was only starting to understand about Rae. "Mom said I should be a teacher, so when I went to college, I chose something as far from teaching as possible."

"You do work with kids."

She shook her head and folded her arms. "No, I organize programs for kids. I'm not coaching or directly involved in influencing them at all."

"You like your job, though, right?"

"Sure, love my job."

"And your mom? You two are close, I thought."

"Yeah, sure. Now."

He nodded a couple of times and stepped toward her. He ran his fingers down the side of her face, glad when she seemed to relax and the negative emotions in her eyes melted into something more like desire. "Sorry about your dad."

She shrugged that one shoulder again, driving Ben's pulse toward the ceiling. "It's okay."

"You don't know where he is now?"

"He stayed for that summer and left again. Totally broke my mother's heart all over again. Not a birthday card since." Her voice held a loud note of pain in the last sentence, and Ben slipped his fingers into hers.

"You want Capone again?"

Her honeyed, brown eyes calmed and she smiled. "Of course I want Capone again."

Ben gave her half a smile. "You know where he is." He watched her take the few steps to Capone's stall and enter like she'd done it a thousand times before. She really was a natural with a horse, but he wasn't going to tell her that. He wanted her in the saddle next to him, on the farm beside him.

Admiration for Rae washed through him, and Ben recognized the feeling of falling. He'd been in this tailspin exactly once before, but then it had been terrible. An out-of-control terrible. The day he found out his parents had died, he'd fallen.

Falling in love felt eerily similar—uncertainty for the future. Confusion over how he felt. But this time, he found himself smiling about the free-fall, which was scary and exciting at the same time.

———

BY THE TIME BEN AND RAE RETURNED FROM THEIR RIDE AND headed toward the farmhouse hand-in-hand, Missy and Tucker had already arrived. Ben knew, because the familiar sound of Fritz's barks echoed around the silent farm.

"That's Missy's dog," he said, taking a detour around the house to the front yard instead of entering it. Sure enough, Tucker stood near the driveway and tossed a ball. Fritz and Rambo tore after it, with Fritz catching it in midair before veering back to Tucker. The dog dropped the ball at Tucker's feet and barked. Barked. Barked.

Rambo sat down, his tongue lolling out of his mouth sideways and his tail thumping the grass. Tucker threw the ball again.

"Hey, Tucker," Ben said.

Tucker turned toward him. "There you are."

"Are we late?" Ben looked toward the farmhouse.

"Missy insisted we come early. She wanted to talk to Rae."

"I'll go in." Rae gave Ben a smile, removed her hand from his, and maneuvered through the dog fray toward the front porch.

"Sorry," Ben said. "You guys always come at five. I thought we had plenty of time."

Tucker threw the ball and settled his weight on his back leg. "We do. You know how Missy gets." He grinned at Ben. "You take Rae out into the woods?"

Ben ducked his head. He didn't have a lot of experience with women, but even he knew better than to kiss and tell. "Yeah. It's peaceful out there."

Tucker nodded. "That it is."

"Sometimes I just skip church and spend the day in the woods, with my horse."

"No better place to commune with God."

Ben exhaled and looked out over the horizon. In the distance, the blurred edge of Island Park sat. Ben had been in a lot of rural locations. Farms in the middle of Idaho. Ranches in the wilds of Montana. Corrals at the base of mountains, without any other people around. He'd always felt close to the Lord under the clear, clean sky.

He'd always gone alone when he needed to find his center again. He'd always spent a lot of time thinking about his parents and expressing his gratitude for Sam. But today, he'd spent his time talking to and thinking about Rae. Kissing Rae. Holding her hand and laughing with her.

He felt just as centered. Gratitude descended on him and he said, "Thanks, Tucker."

"For what?"

Ben met the older man's eye. And though Tucker had lots of money, and owned the farm, and held more experience and wisdom in his pinky finger than Ben had in his whole body, Ben didn't feel as inadequate as he normally did.

"For this job." He smiled, and the gesture wobbled a little on his face. "For everything."

Tucker seemed to know Ben meant more than he was able to say. "Missy made lasagna *and* her banana maple cake. She's probably spitting fire by now. Let's go eat."

"Banana maple cake? She really did go all out." Ben laughed, truly realizing for the first time how many good people he had surrounding him.

"Well, I don't eat fruit, so she has to do something with all those black bananas." He patted his completely flat stomach. "I've gained ten pounds since we've been married." He opened the door and waited for Ben to enter the farmhouse.

"Feel free to bring banana maple cake to the farm any time." Ben entered the house, his heart tumbling through his chest at the glorious sight of Rae laughing in the kitchen with Missy. Of course he knew she'd be there.

He was just real glad about it.

14

Rae experienced something great right there at Steeple Ridge Farm, the place she'd abandoned almost two decades earlier. She remembered the charm of the horses, the calm atmosphere out in the pastures, the sense of peace that could only be found in the green leaves of the trees in the forest. Unless it was fall, and the orange, yellow, and red leaves were on the trees. Then *that* was the most magical, wonderful time to be in the forest atop a horse.

The table in the kitchen had room for four chairs, but someone had shoved seven around it, making the space cozy and comfortable.

"All right." Sam entered the kitchen and clapped his hands. "How can I help?"

"Sit down," Missy said. "The food is ready." She cut a glance at Ben and Tucker as they came into the farmhouse, laughter in their voices and happiness in the very air around them. "Time to eat," she said louder.

Ben filled the kitchen with his presence, bringing one arm around her waist and pulling her close. "Hey." He acted like he hadn't seen her in days, not only a few minutes.

Two more Buttars men burst through the back door, which slammed into the wall and rattled the windows.

"Hey, hey!" Sam said. "This is our house."

"My house," Tucker said.

"Sorry, boss," the darkest-haired one said. He glanced at Rae. "Oh, hello, Miss Cantwell." She giggled as he bowed at the waist. "We'll wash up and be right back."

"Which one's which?" she asked as both men moved down the hall to the bathroom.

"The one that just spoke to you is Logan," Ben said. "He's the dog-lover. You two would get along great."

"And the other is Darren."

"Right."

"Come sit," Missy barked, and Rae didn't dare to disobey her. She marched over to a seat at the table and sat. Ben joined her, and Sam took the spot beside him. Tucker sat on the other side of Rae, and Missy leaned over the table and set a massive pan of lasagna in the center. She glanced behind her. "What is taking them so long?"

Tucker put his hand on her back and said, "Sit down, sweetheart. They're coming."

Rae noticed the way she looked at him, the way he calmed her, the special way they could communicate without speaking. She'd seen the same look between others of her married friends, and she'd always longed for it for herself.

She deliberately didn't look at Ben as his brothers came bustling down the hall, chuckling about something only the two of them knew about. They brought incredible energy with them, and as Rae glanced around at the people at the table, she felt an overwhelming amount of love.

Love between brothers. Love between Tucker and Missy. Fierce friendship between the brothers and Missy and Tucker. Rae was the newcomer here, but she barely felt like it.

Tucker said grace, and Ben gave her hand an extra squeeze

before picking up his fork. They talked about what Pastor Gray had said, the different horses on the farm, how Gladys Bright was doing. The conversation was easy and boisterous, often with multiple topics going on at the same time. Rae told Sam about her work at the rec center, she and Ben talked about Capone, Missy asked her about her mom.

By the time the banana maple cake made an appearance, Rae thought she would explode with happiness. Missy had definitely improved her baking skills beyond the frozen pizzas with extra cheese that Rae had eaten as a teenager.

Rae had never seen a cake get consumed so fast. But with five men at the table, the dessert went from glazed to perfection to crumbs on a sheet tray in only a few minutes. She couldn't complain; she had two squares of the treat herself, along with a steaming cup of coffee with more cream than she normally allowed herself.

"Thank you, Missy," she said, true sincerity in her voice. "It was so good to see you." She hugged her friend and helped her stack all the dishes. Rae noticed that Missy didn't take any of the leftovers with her but boxed them up and put them in the brothers' fridge. Sam and Ben helped carry the pans out to Tucker's truck while Logan and Darren loaded the dishwasher.

Without a chore, Rae picked up the ball Tucker had been throwing to the dogs earlier and held it up while Fritz barked. "All right." She tossed the ball and the two dogs ran after it.

Ben returned before Fritz did, and they settled on the front steps, their hands intertwined. "That was great," she said.

"You think so?"

"Why wouldn't I think so?"

"We're...loud. Eat too fast. Talk with our mouths full." Ben shrugged. "Sunday is the only day we actually use real plates. Did Missy tell you that?"

"Sunday is the only day I actually cook," she admitted. "And it's usually with my mother."

He glanced at her. "Now I feel bad."

"Why?"

"You should've invited your mom too. She had to eat alone today?"

"She doesn't mind." Rae threw the ball again and focused on the clouds drifting through the evening sky. "She eats alone every night."

She felt Ben's frown though she wasn't looking at him. Maybe he'd been able to tell she hadn't told the whole truth.

"Fine," she said. "I sometimes go over there during the week, take her a sandwich from the diner or something."

"Does Harry make vegetarian sandwiches?"

Rae groaned. "Unfortunately."

His hand squeezed hers as he chuckled. He bent over and picked up the ball when Rambo dropped it at his feet. "So Missy said the horseback riding thing isn't going to happen."

Rae's overly full stomach jumped. "I don't have time."

"Missy's summer camps are already full," he said.

"That's what she said."

"I'm not sure why she thought the rec center needed to sponsor the lessons then."

"It was a good idea," Rae said. "And we like to offer a wide variety of programs for our families."

"Maybe in the fall," he said. "She said you'd be less busy then."

"The farm is busy in the fall," Rae said. "That's show season." She exhaled. "Missy's always loved this farm."

"I love this farm too." Ben's voice sounded reverent, causing Rae to glance at him.

"It does have something special about it." Rae watched Tucker climb in the truck, tuck Missy into his side, and back up. Sam wandered back to the front porch, a relaxed look on his face. For a moment, she thought he might sit right on down beside her.

Instead, he grinned at them and said, "Family meeting at eight-thirty, Ben. That okay?"

"Yeah, I think so."

Rae would have to give him up soon, and she curled further into his side as Sam stepped past them and into the house. The screen door slammed behind him, which made Rae flinch.

"Sorry," Sam called. Then he muttered, "We really need to fix that thing."

Rae giggled, though she had no idea what a family meeting was. "Your brothers are great."

"If there's food around, they do okay."

Rae laughed. "Seriously, I like them."

Ben inhaled deeply, his chest expanding beside her. "Yeah." He sighed. "They're great."

Being a single child had never felt so lonely. She worked up enough saliva to swallow and said, "Sounds like I should go."

"It's barely after seven," he said.

"What do you do at a family meeting?"

Ben swung his attention to her, his eyes navy under the shadows of his hat. "Talk about...family stuff."

Rae nodded like she knew what that meant. She had no idea. "I need to go feed all the cats and dogs."

It was a flimsy excuse, and Rae heard the false notes in her own voice. After all, Ben had just helped her feed everyone several hours ago. She wasn't sure why she was trying to leave. She could spend the next hour simply sitting on the steps, holding Ben's hand, and be happy. They'd managed to fill the many hours between church and dinner without a problem.

But she also realized that she was new in Ben's life. That he had a life without her with his brothers, and she wanted to give them the time together they needed. And maybe, just maybe, she liked her time alone too. Her independence. Her orange-scented house with two little dogs who would curl up on either side of her while she watched a movie.

She inhaled deeply as she stood. "I need to go."

"All right." Ben stood too and took her face in his hands. He gazed down at her, the closeness and connection between them so intimate, Rae's heartbeat skyrocketed at the same time she smiled. Ben kissed her, the pressure of his lips against hers gentle and insistent at the same time. She lost herself inside his touch, her head a bit fuzzy when he pulled back.

"See you later," he said, his voice husky and hoarse.

"Yeah." Rae couldn't articulate much more than that, and she drifted away from Ben and to her car, on a high that would definitely last the several days until she could see him again.

———

FOR SOME REASON RAE COULDN'T NAME, SHE COULDN'T STAND TO be in the office, so she spent the first few days of the week at the Sports Complex with her crew. She mowed lawns and swept wood chips back into the playground area. She raked sand on ball fields and ate trashy junk food lunches from the gas station down the street from the outdoor facility.

On Thursday, she sent Burke, Len, and Eli for lunch at The Bread Company on Main Street. They made triple-decker sandwiches on homemade honey wheat bread that made Rae's eyes roll back in her head with deliciousness. And salads. And soups. She and her guys ordered three dozen sandwiches, chips, and drinks, and settled at the tables in the pavilion to eat.

A sense of family and community existed among her crew, and though she was the only woman, Rae didn't feel out of place here either. She'd eaten half her sandwich and wrapped the rest for dinner when Burke said, "Rae."

She found him nodding toward the parking lot, where a tall, broad man wearing cowboy boots and his signature black cowboy hat strode toward them. A car that looked a lot like

Missy's was driving away. Rae's face broke into a smile and she climbed out from the picnic table.

"Ben." She almost squealed, but managed to keep it to a joyful laugh. He picked her up and swung her around, setting her on her feet and kissing her right there in front of her entire crew. Cat calls and whistles filled the air, and Rae tipped her head back and laughed.

She turned back to her guys and towed Ben with her into the shaded pavilion. "So this is...." She glanced at him, at the flush in his face that surely had nothing to do with the mid-day heat. "My boyfriend, Ben." She squeezed his hand, suddenly aware of how stinky she probably was. How underdressed to be entertaining her *boyfriend*.

She glanced down at her dark brown T-shirt that said "Forget love. I'd rather fall in chocolate" across the front. Ratty jeans with holes in both knees. Hair tucked into a messy bun. Manly work boots.

"Do we have any extra sandwiches?" she asked, and three were lifted in the air. "Have you eaten lunch?"

"Lunch would be great."

Burke came forward and introduced himself to Ben, taking him from Rae and into the fray of the crew. Ben seemed to fit with the other men just fine, and Rae tucked her hands in her back pockets and grinned at the back of his cowboy hat, the only thing that made him stand out among the crowd.

She just hoped it was too hot for any bees to be out, because then Ben would stay.

15

M y boyfriend, Ben.
  Boyfriend, Ben.
  Boyfriend, boyfriend, boyfriend.

Ben had no idea how to be a boyfriend, but maybe showing up at the Sports Complex during Rae's lunch because he couldn't stand to go another hour without kissing her was a good start. He hadn't told her that. Hadn't said anything to her at all before simply sweeping her into his arms, where she fit, where she belonged, and kissing her.

She was the one who'd applied the label. Changed his life for what felt like the tenth time this month.

He bit into a ham and turkey sandwich on thick slabs of sourdough and groaned. "This is fantastic," he said around the mouthful of food.

"Bread Company," one of the men said. "Best bread in town."

"Ben makes soft pretzels," Rae said, sitting backward next to him on the bench. He glanced at her, a smile automatically springing to his face. He liked her in pencil skirts and fancy blouses, but this jeans and T-shirt and sunglasses look also suited her. His blood raged like fire no matter how much cold soda he swallowed.

"Soft pretzels?" Burke asked. "Well, I think we'd all like to try those."

"I can bring some into town next week," Ben said. "Sam— that's my brother—says we're taking a few days off at the farm next week." He kept his gaze on Rae for a few extra seconds, remembering why he'd come to see her. "We're going to Wyoming over the weekend for Memorial Day."

Her eyebrows stretched toward her hairline. "That sounds fun."

It didn't sound fun to Ben. He didn't know what to expect in Wyoming. Sam had taken the brothers to the ranch where he'd been working when his parents' plane went down, and only Sam had been back to the farmhouse and dual graves on the property. Ben had never gone. Had never even asked to go.

But at the family meeting on Sunday, Sam had suggested they all go to Wyoming for Memorial Day, check on the house, perhaps see what they needed to do to get it ready to sell, put flowers on the graves. Ben hadn't been sleeping well since agreeing to go. He wasn't sure why. Only that he had a nest of bees in his abdomen that flew into a frenzy when he thought about returning to the farm where he'd spent the first fifteen years of his life.

And if he got stung by one of those bees....

He finished the sandwich he'd been given and met Rae's eye. "Want to walk?"

She stood as an answer and Ben took her hand in his as they walked away from the pavilion. "Your guys are nice," he said. He was glad that some of his jealousy hadn't even reared. The man he'd come face-to-face with at Rae's hadn't been there, and maybe Ben just didn't like him all that much.

"They are."

"I like your shirt."

"I like your hat." She laughed and skipped a few paces ahead of him, turning around and walking backward. "You nervous about going to Wyoming?"

He nodded, the insects taking up residence in his throat, choking him. Glancing around, he looked for physical bees, almost wishing to find some. Then he could leave this park and take Rae with him.

"Have you been back since they died?"

He shook his head, relieved Rae seemed to already know all of the things he was worried about.

"When are you leaving?"

"Tomorrow," he said. "I texted you this morning, but you must not have your phone with you."

"It's in the shed." She rejoined him at his side. "Is the...well, I just called you my boyfriend. I couldn't quite tell how you felt about that."

He stopped walking and turned toward her, a smile edging out the tension in his muscles. "I liked it. I liked it a whole lot." He leaned down and touched his lips to hers. She clung to him and kissed him back with the same careful passion he'd experienced over the weekend.

"Good," she whispered. "Because I like you a whole lot."

Ben couldn't help kissing her again, even if his lips didn't quite line up with hers, as curved as they were. "Sam gave me the rest of the day off," he said as they started walking again. "So put me to work. What do you need help with around here?"

"We'll have to ask Burke."

"Aren't you the boss?"

"I'm more of the big-picture person. Burke handles all the details."

"So he tells you what to do?" Ben scoffed. "I find that hard to believe."

She looked up at him and even through her sunglasses he felt the laser in her gaze. "Why's that?"

"Because." He waved his free hand, the bees in his chest rioting for an entirely different reason now. "You're the boss."

She stopped at a fork in the path. Left would take them around the park and eventually back to the pavilion. Right went around the ball fields and toward the parking lot.

"I'm not *your* boss," she said.

Ben had no idea how to be a boyfriend. What to say that would erase the straight line on her shoulders or ease the tension in her jaw. He didn't know how to flirt very well. So when he said, "Sure you are, Rae," and smiled, he had no idea if he was headed for a breakup or another kiss. "I'll do whatever you want," he added in a voice so low the air barely rumbled with sound.

She ducked her head, a smile slipping across her face. "I want you to take me to dinner tonight."

"Done."

"I want you to stay and watch a movie with me until it's almost midnight."

A tremor ran through Ben, and not only at the thought of spending so much time alone with Rae, in her house, the site of their first kiss. "There's nothing I'd rather do."

"What do you want?" she asked.

"I want you to call me tomorrow night." He swallowed. "I might not answer, because Sam did the itinerary and everything. But I know I'm gonna want to talk to you."

"Sure, I can do that." She guided him to the left. "You can talk to Sam, right? Does he understand how you're feeling about going back to Wyoming?"

The knot in Ben's throat loosened. "Yeah, he does. He seems to know without me saying anything. We haven't talked about it much. I just—" Ben stopped talking, because he couldn't quite classify how he felt. "I want you to kiss me," he said. "Like you did that first time in your kitchen."

She tipped up onto her toes. "Your wish is my command." She pressed her mouth to his, and Ben held her tight, finally able to stop obsessing about what he might or might not see, feel, hear, or understand in Wyoming.

———

BEFORE BEN KNEW IT, HE WAS WALKING INTO THE AIRPORT IN NEW York City, the noise and crowd almost more than he could stand. His life for the past decade hadn't included a lot of people, or the bustling, pulsing atmosphere of a city, and he hardly knew in which direction to focus.

No one else seemed to be wearing a cowboy hat, but none of his brothers removed theirs so Ben didn't either. They each towed a rolling carry-on bag behind them, enough to get through three days out of town. Ben wished he could pack courage and patience as easily as he could deodorant and shaving cream.

As it was, he found himself finding the music he'd down-loaded onto his phone and sticking in a pair of ear buds to keep from snapping at Logan's and Darren's antics. Didn't they realize everyone was already staring at the country cowboys from Vermont?

The sound of guitars strumming and drums playing soothed him, and he finally understood why Rae blasted rock music through her house before going to work in the mornings. Music could turn off the mind, make it settle, force the thoughts into silence.

Sometime later Sam tapped his shoulder and indicated that they were boarding. Ben swallowed and stood. He hadn't flown before. Ever. Sam had shown up on the farm in Wyoming with the truck. They'd loaded everything they could fit for four men and left. That truck had been all over the country before they'd landed in Vermont.

Ben found he couldn't get his feet to move toward the gate.

Logan and Darren disappeared down the hall like it was no big deal to fly. No problem that their parents had perished on an airplane.

"C'mon," Sam said. "It's okay, Ben."

Ben met his brother's eyes, panic rearing beneath his breastbone. Why hadn't they talked about this? Intellectually, Ben had known they'd be flying to Billings. But it hadn't been real until this moment.

"This is a real big plane," Sam said. "It's not like the one Mom and Dad were on." He touched Ben's arm. "Come on, Ben. It's okay." He spoke in the soothing voice he used when breaking horses, and though Ben had known Sam possessed a rare talent when it came to calming horses, it meant something different now.

"I need a drink," Ben said over a scratchy throat.

Sam lifted the bottle of water he held in his hand. Ben gulped it, hoping for the liquid to calm the storm raging in his stomach. It didn't really, but after draining the last drop, he was able to take a step toward the desk. Then another. And another.

With Sam behind him, occasionally whispering an encouragement, Ben finally made it to his aisle seat. He couldn't even fathom sitting next to the window and being able to see out and down. Down, down, down.

He pressed his eyes closed, willing the time to pass in an instant. Focusing on his breathing, he made it through the preflight instructions, the take off, and the beverage service. Only then did he allow himself to relax enough to be able to fall asleep.

———

BEN'S LEGS WERE STILL SHAKY, EVEN AFTER SAM HAD GOTTEN THE keys to the rental car and everyone had piled into the mid-size

SUV. The town of Coral Canyon sat nestled against the base of the eastern edge of Yellowstone National Park, a couple of hours south of Billings. Memories flooded Ben as the terrain he hadn't seen for a decade seemed familiar and comforting to him.

It helped that Logan said things like, "Remember how we used to ride our bikes out to the swimming hole?" and Darren would answer with, "You always made me carry both fishing poles."

Ben had tagged along after his older brothers his whole life, and he'd always packed the sunblock the twins had forgotten. Logan would rip off a piece of his sandwich and a piece of Darren's so Ben had something to eat, and he'd say, "Don't stare at the girls when they show up."

Because no matter where Logan and Darren went, beautiful girls seemed to follow. Even as teenagers. Ben had always been infatuated by them and when it was finally his turn to meet pretty girls at the swimming hole, he'd only had the opportunity to get to know one. Then his life had been turned upside down and inside out.

The town of Coral Canyon itself hadn't seemed to change much. It had felt bigger as a child, but Ben estimated it to be slightly larger than Island Park, with several blocks of very touristy shops, restaurants, and art galleries. Behind that, the real town breathed, with farms, quaint houses, and pastures full of cows, horses, chickens, and pigs.

The rusted steel moose his mother had loved still stood guard outside the ritziest gallery, and Ben could hear his mother's high-pitched voice saying she was going to own it one day. A burst of sadness exploded through him at the realization that at least one of her dreams hadn't come true. He wondered how many others she'd given up to raise four boys on the outskirts of a tiny mountain town while her husband planted and plowed.

The commercial area got swallowed by lane after lane of

houses, until finally Sam turned left and headed down the last road leading south into the forest. A mile down the road, the farmhouse where Ben had grown up came into view. The blue paint seemed darker now than he remembered, but the lawn was neat and trimmed. The windows clear. The front porch railing shone so white Ben knew it had been recently painted.

Someone had been living here. Or at least taking care of the place.

Sam pulled into the driveway and bumped down the dirt tire tracks with the emerald green grass growing in between. He put the SUV in park, but no one moved to get out. All four brothers stared at the house, the yard, the garden plot to the right, lost inside their own heads.

Ben finally moved. He pulled the door latch and stepped into the heat of the Wyoming day. The air smelled like pine and fresh water, and he took a deep, deep breath of it, realizing it had always been a part of him and always would be.

How he'd loved Wyoming. His breath hitched, but he forced himself to step toward the front door. As a kid, he never used the front door. If someone knocked there or rang the doorbell, they were strangers to the Buttars.

Everyone knew to climb the six steps and enter the kitchen on the right side of the house. Without a back door, that side entrance was used for everything. Hauling groceries in. Taking water out to the animals in the barn. One particularly nasty winter, Ben's dad had constructed the roof of a garage he intended to finish when the temperatures weren't below freezing. But a wind storm had come that spring and knocked the bare wood beams to the ground, narrowly missing taking out part of the house in the process.

Ben approached the front door, knowing fullwell what sat on the other side. A formal living room, which housed his mother's prized possession—her grandmother's piano. His mom had taught piano lessons in that living room, and none of the boys were allowed in there if it wasn't their assigned time to practice. All but Sam had quit by the time they were twelve, and a pinch started behind Ben's left eye. Had his mother been upset that none of her sons loved to play the piano the way she did?

He put his hand on the doorknob, the shape of it familiar and foreign at the same time.

"Ben," Sam said.

He turned to find Sam at the bottom of the porch, his hand on the railing. Just three steps and he'd be next to Ben.

"Can we go in?" Ben asked. "Who's been taking care of the place?"

"I've been paying the Steadman's to look after the farm. They took the animals when we left, and they had a half-dozen sons to come mow the lawn and check on the house."

Ben remembered the Steadmans. With eight children, they were hard to forget. And they were the closest family to the Buttars' farm, which meant the boys played together whether they liked each other or not.

Ben had liked them. "Davy was my age," he said, turning back to the door. "Their youngest has to be...what? Sixteen or seventeen by now?"

Sam took those three steps and joined Ben on the front porch. "He's graduating from high school next week. He won't be able to take care of the farm anymore."

Ben looked at his oldest brother. "That's why we're here. That's why you're thinking of selling it."

The usual strength in Sam's shoulders disappeared. "You're close, Ben." Logan and Darren joined them on the porch. "But I'm not thinking of selling it." He glanced from brother to brother. "I'm thinking about moving back here and running it."

The idea seemed utterly ridiculous to Ben. He twisted the knob and stepped inside the house.

The brown carpet stretched before him, giving way to beige tile that extended right into the kitchen and left down a hallway.

The piano stood in its rightful spot, and Ben trailed his fingers over the ivory, sending discordant notes into the air.

Everyone spread out, examining little bits and pieces of the house that held special memories for them. Ben found a single box of baking soda in the fridge, and then he went downstairs to where he and his brothers had bedrooms. Logan and Darren had always shared, but Ben had enjoyed his own space, especially after Sam had moved out, gone on to the ranch in Montana.

Everything was exactly how they'd left it that last day in August. Fully furnished, the house had simply kept, the way Sam had said it would. As Ben looked in room after room, the thought of coming back here and continuing his father's farm didn't seem so far-fetched after all.

An hour later, the brothers sat in a booth at Sam's favorite restaurant. "We have a lot to talk about," he said. "I've handled everything the past ten years, because I had to. Logan and Darren were barely adults, and Ben barely got to stay with us as it was."

The waitress arrived and everyone placed their orders. Sam waited until she was far enough away not to overhear. "Mom and Dad had a will. They left the farm to me." He took a big breath. "But I'm willing to talk about selling it. Or letting one of you have it if you want it." He glanced around the table, and though his eyes were serious, they held more concern than anything else.

"I don't want it," Ben said first. "I'm happy in Island Park, at Steeple Ridge."

Logan looked at Darren, who stared right back. "You should have it, Sam," Darren finally said. "You've always loved the farm, and Dad left it to you."

Sam nodded, dropping his eyes to the tabletop. Ben couldn't tell if that was the answer he'd wanted or not. "Tucker doesn't really need me at Steeple Ridge. It's just that...Wyoming is a long way from Vermont." He trained his gaze on Ben. "And there's more. We each got an inheritance. I've been managing the money, because we've been together, but I think that's all about to change."

Ben squirmed. His closest brother and best friend was Sam. How could Ben stay in Vermont if Sam came back to Coral Canyon? It didn't feel right.

"I've been paying the Steadman's out of the estate. But we all get our inheritance when we get married."

Ben sucked in a breath and held it. Logan said, "We do? Why didn't you tell us that? I may have been trying harder to get married."

Sam chuckled and elbowed Logan. "No, you wouldn't have."

Logan laughed, always the most laid back of the brothers. "No, probably not."

"How much is it?" Darren asked.

"A lot." Sam shrugged. "I hired an investor while we were still at the ranch in Montana. He's coming to meet with us at the house tomorrow. We'll all know more then." He took his drink when the waitress set it down and didn't wait for her to leave before he added, "I had a realtor coming too, but I think we can probably cancel that."

"So you'll be moving right away?" Ben asked, his heart doing loops around his chest.

Sympathy shone in Sam's eyes. "I don't know, Ben."

The food arrived and the conversation seemed to be over. At least until Sam said, "But I have a guess as to which of us will be getting married first." The teasing sparkle in his eye was aimed directly at Ben, and the brotherly ribbing about Rae started.

Ben didn't mind. He even threw fuel on the fire by saying, "She called me her boyfriend in front of her crew yesterday," which really set Logan's teasing to the next level.

Ben just shook his head, appreciating the closeness and camaraderie with his brothers—who were also his best friends. A pinch of sadness started just at the bottom of his heart at the thought that Sam was considering coming back to the farm while the rest of the brothers returned to Vermont.

He laughed, the warm sound filling the diner easily. Ben caught the sound and tried to memorize it, so that if Sam did come to Coral Canyon for good, Ben would be able to remember him by his best feature.

16

Rae drove home after church on Sunday and almost didn't get over to her mother's. In the end, she walked the several blocks in an attempt to psyche herself up to be with other people. She hadn't realized how much she'd come to rely on Ben for conversation. She'd only met him a month ago, but she'd gotten used to sending him a text and having it returned almost immediately.

She'd talked to him a couple of times since he'd left for Wyoming, but each conversion had been hushed and hurried, and he'd ended the call almost as soon as he'd answered. He was clearly busy and overwhelmed with a whole part of his life she knew nothing about.

"Knock, knock," she said as she opened her mom's front door. The smell of curry hit her, and Rae sent a prayer of thanksgiving heavenward. At least her mom had made something delicious today, as if she'd somehow sensed Rae needed familiarity.

Her mom came down the hall wearing a smile. "There you are. I was just about to call Kevin to go find you. Thought you might be in a ditch on the side of the road."

Rae laughed at the thought of the Sherriff trying to locate

anyone. "Mom, Kevin's half-blind." She stepped around her mom's cats and entered the kitchen. "And there aren't any ditches between here and my house." She grinned at her mom.

"You've been going out to the farm a lot." Her mom gave her a cocked eyebrow.

"Yeah." Rae sat at the bar. "I'm dating Ben Buttars." The words didn't sound real, but the way her heart pulsed at the thought of Ben's large hands cradling her face certainly did.

"I thought you were taking a boyfriend break." She lifted the lid on the wild rice and curry soup, filling the whole house with the scent of chicken and salt.

"I was." Rae got up and retrieved two bowls from the cupboard. "I can't help when I met Ben."

"You're feeling good about him?"

"Very good." Rae nudged her mom to the side with a playful hipcheck. "But if I don't eat some of this soup in the next thirty seconds, I might starve to death."

Chuckling, her mom pulled a bag of potato rolls from the bread drawer. Rae sighed happily, determined to eat an entire day's worth of calories in this one meal.

———

TUESDAY MORNING DAWNED WITH THE PROMISE OF RAIN. RAE LOVED the cooler temperatures and cracked the sliding glass door, positioning a box in front of it so the pets couldn't escape. She showered, blasting her loud rock music from every speaker in the smart house, and poured herself a steaming cup of coffee as her breakfast.

She'd taken one sip when she saw Cherry-Pop and Betty Boop sitting in front of their food bowls. "Sorry guys." She got everyone fed, but Cherry and Betty didn't move. She followed their gazes and looked into the backyard. "What is it?"

The neighbors behind her and to the east had fences, but Rae just had pine trees on the west. "Where's Ralph?" The box didn't look like it had been moved, but Rae started a thorough search of the house for the missing coon cat.

She couldn't find him. As her panic grew, her options dwindled. She needed to get to work, and she didn't have any more time to search for Ralph. She left the sliding glass door open and sent a quick text to Ben—*I know you're not working today. I lost Ralph. Can you come meet me at lunch to search for him?*—before heading over to the rec center.

She felt like someone had poured Mexican jumping beans into her blood. Tears pressed behind her eyes at the thought of something happening to Ralph. Half-deaf and without a way to defend himself, he could get seriously injured if he came across a stray dog.

Rae made it into her office only to be pulled out a moment later when Meredith walked by to say, "There you are. The meeting about the aquatic center started ten minutes ago. Zack sent me to find you. Upstairs in room two-oh-one."

She flew up the stairs, knowing the proposal for an expanded swimming pool needed her support in order to pass. She'd promised Zack she'd be there, even detail how it could benefit the Sports Complex and the youth recreation programs.

She took precious seconds to smooth her hair and take one, two controlled breaths before entering the conference room. "Sorry I'm late."

Zack speared her with a look of half-gratitude, half-annoyance. No one else seemed to mind that she'd come in tardy. It barely looked like they'd started anyway. But it was clear which side of the table she needed to sit on. Those who didn't want any more tax dollars spent on the aquatic center had folders spread in front of them, their faces drawn with downturned lines.

She slipped around to the other side of the table, where Zack sat with a couple of City Council members, sans folders and frowns.

At the front of the room, the Sports Director had a map on the board, and he continued to detail where the money would be spent, on what, and why it was necessary.

Rae couldn't concentrate on anything that took longer than two seconds to say, which was everything. Her left leg kept bouncing, bouncing, bouncing, until Zack finally put his hand on her knee. That innocent gesture sent her emotions straight to her head, and she jumped to her feet.

"Excuse me." She strode toward the stairs and down them, despite Zack's calls behind her. She just needed to get to her office. She could call Layla; the vet would go look for Ralph. She ran the last few steps and almost had the door closed when Zack muscled his way inside.

"What's wrong?" he asked.

"I lost Ralph," Rae blurted as she searched frantically for her phone. Where had she put it? She pulled open a desk drawer though she literally kept nothing in there besides lip gloss and Chapstick. "I need to call Layla. Ralph is a house cat. He can't be outside." She froze. "What if he's already hurt?" She swiped her keys off her desk, giving up on the phone. "I need to go find him."

"Rae." Zack put his hands on her shoulders. "You're not being reasonable. He's probably just in the backyard. Or in one of those huge trees in your yard."

A tear slipped down her face. "He's my responsibility." She didn't take animals she couldn't care for. That was why she'd forbidden Layla from bringing any homeless pets to their dinner and bunko nights.

Not that they'd been getting together much lately. With Rae's work schedule, and her new relationship with Ben, she spent every spare minute with him.

"Come on, now." Zack gathered her into his chest and held her tight. "Don't cry."

Rae couldn't help it. She didn't spend a lot of time crying, but the tears slipped down her face easily now. And it felt good to have this emotional release. Good, after a weekend alone, worried about Ben in Wyoming and how he was feeling and what demons he'd been facing.

The sound of boots echoing on the concrete hall registered in her ears at the same time Ben appeared in her office doorway. His face moved from scared and sympathetic to furious and fierce in under a second.

Rae didn't have time to sniffle, breathe, or move before he turned and stormed away, the boot steps ten times as loud as they'd been previously.

"Ben!" she called, disentangling herself from Zack's embrace and rushing into the hall. All she saw was his retreating back.

"Ben!' she tried again, hurrying after him.

He paused near Meredith, said something that took less than a moment, and marched out of the rec center.

17

Ben had heard Rae calling his name. A more mature—and less jealous—man would turn and wait for her to catch up. Explain. Something.

But Ben didn't feel mature right now. Or calm. His brother was moving more than halfway across the country and he'd found his girlfriend in the arms of another man.

Ben cast the still-cooling soft pretzels on the seat beside him a nasty glare. He'd gotten up at the crack of dawn the way he normally did though he wasn't working the farm today. Just to make the pretzels for Rae and her crew. He'd planned to surprise them mid-afternoon for a two-thirty pick-me-up.

Then he'd gotten Rae's text right as the last batch of pretzels came out of the oven. He'd only taken a few minutes to bag everything up and grab a bottle of ketchup and one of mustard before grabbing the keys to the truck and hitting the road.

He'd checked her house first—she hadn't been home. But Ralph was, and Ben had been able to coax him into the house with the nub of a pretzel. The cat was safe, and Ben wanted to tell Rae in person. Hold her. Kiss her. Feed her pretzels by candlelight.

His chest pinched and bruised. He shook his head. "You're immature, jealous, and stupid," he muttered to himself. Just because Rae called him her boyfriend didn't mean they were getting married. He'd known her for a month. Thirty days. He barely knew what he knew about her, let alone all the things he didn't know.

He roared into the parking lot at the Sports Complex and barely had the truck out of gear before leaping from it. He reached back in and snatched the pretzels from the seat, along with the condiments. The pavilion wasn't full of men the way it had been last week, but it didn't take him long to find someone.

"Hey, Ben," he said, and Ben vaguely remembered seeing him at lunch last week.

"I brought the pretzels for the crew," he said. "Can I just give them to you? Rae said something about a shed...." He glanced toward the corner of the park, where the shed was currently concealed by trees.

"Yeah, sure." The man accepted the bags of pretzels. "I can radio to everyone, let them know to come get one before they go today."

Ben managed a weak smile. "Thanks." He needed to get out of there before Rae showed up. He'd given Meredith a pretzel on the way in, and he'd said, "I got Ralph back inside," without stopping on the way out. He figured Rae would demand to know everything he'd said to Meredith, and she'd tell about the pretzels, the cat, the complete one-eighty in mood.

It wouldn't take Rae long to run home and check on Ralph. She'd put two and two together, and she could be at the Sports Complex at any moment. Ben didn't want to be there when she showed up.

He also didn't want to return to Steeple Ridge so soon. Sam wouldn't expect him back for hours, and Ben didn't feel much like seeing him either. Didn't want to explain anything to anyone.

So he set the truck north and drove toward Burlington. Rae

called five minutes outside of town, and Ben found enough maturity to answer the phone with a curt, "Hey."

"Where are you?"

"Driving."

"Driving where?"

He pressed his teeth together. Stayed silent.

Rae's sigh came out in bursts. "The pretzels are still warm."

"I came as soon as I got your text."

"How did you get Ralph back into the house?"

"Turns out all living creatures like pretzels," he said. "Even half-deaf cats."

A half-sob, half-laugh came over the line. "Please come back. Or tell me where you are."

"I'm feeling like ice cream," he said, pressing harder on the accelerator. "I have to go." He hung up before she could argue or say something that would pull hard enough on his heartstrings and make him turn around and go running back to her.

He did want to go running back to her, but the thought also made him feel weak. And he was tired of feeling weak. The entire weekend in Wyoming had tossed all his emotions in a blender set on high. By the time he'd touched down in New York City and then made it back to Steeple Ridge Farm, he could barely tell which way was up.

He'd licked halfway around his peanut butter explosion ice cream cone when the door opened and Rae walked in. Ben almost lost his grip on his treat but managed to keep it from splatting on the table.

Rae spotted him and slid onto the chair across from him. "Hey."

Nerves assaulted him, spreading down into his stomach, where they re-froze the ice cream he'd already swallowed. "Hey."

He'd made it down to the cone before she said, "I was just upset about Ralph."

"I texted you about Ralph."

"I couldn't find my phone."

Ben shook his head and dropped his chin toward his chest so he didn't have to look at Rae. "I don't need excuses."

"What do you need?"

He leveled his gaze at Rae, an intensity building in him he didn't understand. "Are you and Zack a thing?"

"Of course not."

"Do you want to get back together with him?"

"Never." She reached across the table and covered his hand with both of hers. "There's nothing between me and Zack. No spark. There never was, even when we dated."

Ben blinked at her, trying to believe her. "Maybe not for you."

She pulled her hand back. "What does that mean?"

"It means he likes you in a different way than you like him." He sounded like he was still fifteen, still in junior high.

But Rae's eyelids flickered as she blinked. She looked away and leaned back in her chair, crossing her arms. "So what does that mean for us?"

"I have no idea." Ben didn't want to articulate his next words, but he said, "I don't like you working with him, though."

"He's my boss."

"I know exactly who he is." Ben finished his ice cream. "Did you want to get something?"

"I ate three pretzels on the way here." She shot him a half a smile. "Burke is gonna be so mad when he gets back to the shed and finds out I took his snack."

"There were several extras," Ben said. "He should be fine."

Rae's beautiful golden-brown eyes searched his. "I want us to be fine."

Emotion pressed against Ben's vocal chords. He wanted that too, he just couldn't say it. Maybe he needed a day or two to figure out how to rid himself of his jealous tendencies.

"Sam's moving to the farmhouse in Wyoming," he said instead. "And when I get married, I'll inherit almost four hundred thousand dollars." He took a deep breath and told her everything he hadn't been able to tell her over the phone. The fear about flying. The familiarity of Coral Canyon. The forceful way he'd missed his parents so completely that he'd barely been able to eat.

Rae listened. She listened, and at some point, she moved over to his side of the table and curled into his side on the bench seat. She laced her hand through his and laid her head against his shoulder.

He finally finished talking, and the lump in his throat didn't feel so constrictive. "Rae," he said, his voice low in the near-empty ice cream parlor. "I will figure out how to deal with my jealousy, so we can be fine."

"There's absolutely nothing to be jealous of."

"I know," he said. "I know that, I do."

"So will you kiss me now?" She tilted her head to look at him, the teasing glint he enjoyed so much in her eyes.

Ben finally felt grounded enough to smile. "I suppose." He leaned down and pressed his lips to hers, and suddenly, all the envy that had painted his blood green disappeared.

"Don't you look nice?" Behind his brothers, Ben mounted the steps to the church, where Rae waited in all her beauty. She wore a flirty sundress in various shades of teal, which she'd paired with the brightest pair of pink heels he'd ever seen.

He leaned down and she met him halfway for their hello kiss. He didn't want to go inside and find a seat, listen to a sermon. He wanted to take Rae out to the farm, press her against the stall door, and kiss her, kiss her, kiss her.

She giggled, interrupting his fantasy, and turned to enter the church. He went with her, because the thought of not having her hand in his left him feeling hollow and cold. She led him to the row where he always sat with his brothers, and said, "Scootch over, Sam," to the astonishment of Ben.

Sam glanced up and blinked at her before nudging Darren to move down. Rae planted herself between Sam and Ben like she'd done it countless times before. Ben ignored Sam's wide smile and settled his arm around Rae's shoulders.

Pastor Gray stood and started his sermon with, "Addiction is a very real plague, my brothers and sisters. And I don't mean the 'normal' addictions like drugs or alcohol. Addiction can take many forms. Some of us spend too many hours with their hobbies. Some lose their relationships to video games. Some people are workaholics."

Ben felt riveted to the preacher's every word, his gaze and attention unwavering. So much truth dove through him that it felt like the heavens themselves had opened and God himself had spoken from above.

The hour passed in a blink, and Ben shook himself as if he'd been in a trance. To his right, his brothers and Rae had already stood for the final hymn. Ben leapt to his feet, but only one verse remained. He sang it anyway and filed into the aisle with everyone behind him.

The pastor's words bounced around inside his head while he got behind the wheel of Rae's car and drove to her house. He fed the cats and dogs while she went to change. He settled on the couch, exhaustion overcoming him in a way that testified he was coming down with a summer cold.

Beauty jumped onto the couch with him and he tucked her into his chest before closing his eyes. He had no idea how much time had passed before Rae gently shook his shoulder and said, "Ben, we need to go out to the farm."

He blinked, his head foggy and his brain slow. Rae's beautiful face swam before him, eliciting a smile. "Hey." He sat up, dislodging the little white dog from his side. "Sorry." He wiped his hands down his face, trying to get himself fully awake. "What time is it?"

"Almost four."

"Four?" Ben stood and Rae did too. "Wow, I'm more tired than I thought."

"I answered your phone when Sam called," she said. "I told him you'd fallen asleep, and he said you haven't been sleeping well at night."

Ben's defenses rose. "I'm coming down with a little cold. That's all."

Rae cocked her head to the side. "Why aren't you sleeping at night?"

Ben exhaled and searched around the living room for his cowboy hat. "Lots of reasons."

"Name one."

He found his hat and positioned it on his head. "Sam's moving to Wyoming."

"Why does that bother you? He'll be taking care of your family's land. You'd rather sell it?"

"No, I think it's a good move. I'm just going to miss him." Ben picked up her keys and handed them to her. "Can you drive? I'm still a little bit asleep." He tried to smile, but he couldn't quite pull it off.

Rae took the keys from him but didn't make a move toward the exit. "Would you go with him?"

Ben didn't know how to answer, but by the edge in her eyes, what he said would be important. "I don't know what you mean."

"Under normal circumstances, would you be going with him to Wyoming?"

Ben didn't know what "normal circumstances" were, the same way he didn't know how to be a good boyfriend. "If things were normal, we'd all be going with him," Ben said. "That's what we've done for a decade. We've stayed together. Watched out for each other."

Rae nodded, short little bursts of her head. She turned toward the front door, took a couple of steps, and turned back. "But you're adults now."

"Yeah," Ben said because he didn't know what else to say. He and Rae were clearly on two different pages at the moment, and his mind raced for a solution to get back aligned. As he followed Rae out to her car, he realized he wasn't very good at being an adult. That being an adult was actually a lot of hard work, and gratitude that Sam had shielded him for so long poured through Ben.

He settled into the passenger seat and reached for her hand. "Rae," he said. "I wouldn't go with Sam this time, because you're here."

She squeezed his fingers, and Ben was glad he'd finally found the right thing to say. He stared out the window, hearing both truths and lies in the words he'd said. He didn't want to leave Rae in Vermont. But he didn't want Sam to leave Vermont without him either.

18

June passed in a flurry of soccer practices, baseball tournaments, and kisses with Ben. Passionate kisses behind the barn. Sweet kisses under the tree limbs in the forest. Life-changing kisses under the starry sky, late at night, after everyone else had vacated the Sports Complex.

With every day that passed, every text she sent and received from Ben, every new thing she learned about him and revealed about herself, Rae fell a little further in love with him. And she let herself, because it felt safe. He was her safe place, and as June faded into July, she realized he was her best friend.

Ben's jealousies hadn't reared again, and though she'd thought he wasn't being entirely truthful about why he wasn't sleeping, she'd eventually gotten the truth out of him. She wasn't sure Ben even had it in him to lie, and that was something she loved most about it.

Most people enjoyed the time off over the Fourth of July, but Rae worked more hours leading up to that day and on the day itself than any other time of year. Organizing the five-kilometer run fell on her department, and she'd given it to April. It still required a lot of meetings, a slew of texts, and an early morning.

Rae had organized the youth tennis bracket, as well as the adult co-ed softball tournament that ran for the three days leading up to the Fourth, with the championship rounds that afternoon.

Ben had invited her to the grand parade, and Rae said she'd come find him.

She always helped with the 5K run, and she had fifteen minutes to get to the rec center, the starting line for the race. She tucked her debit card in the back pocket of her navy blue shorts and swiped her keys from the kitchen counter. She stepped onto the front porch when her phone went off.

Zack.

She groaned but answered the call with, "I'm on my way."

"Where? The rec center?"

"Yes, I'm ten minutes out." She slid into the driver's seat. "April put me on number distribution."

"I'll call her and tell her she needs someone else. I need you at the Sports Complex."

"What? Why?"

"Just get over here. And bring some boots."

"Boots? Zack—" She cut off, because he'd already hung up. He hadn't sounded happy, but then again, a lot had cooled off in their friendship since the incident in her office. She hadn't said anything to Zack, but he'd somehow gotten the memo that she had a new boyfriend now and it wasn't him.

She got back out of the car and hurried into the house to grab her work boots. They clashed with her navy shorts, and red and white striped tank top. She wore sparkly star-shaped earrings and bright red lipstick to complete the patriotic ensemble. And her brown, muddy, man-boots simply didn't fit.

She stewed over what she would possibly find at the Sports Complex as she drove. She went around to the shed side, where she'd be able to park closer and hopefully find Zack. Dialing as she got out of the car, she had him on the line before she entered the shed.

"All right, I'm here." She pushed into the shed and found nothing out of the ordinary. "Where are you?" She turned back to the facility, only seeing where the pond used to be, and the lovely green leaves of the trees.

"Ball fields. Don't worry, I have maintenance on the way."

Rae started around the path. "Maintenance? What's going on?" The urge to run almost choked her, but she kept herself at a brisk walk. She rounded the bend and didn't need Zack to answer verbally.

The water shooting fifty feet into the air was like a scream in her soul.

She hung up and broke into a run, not that she could fix the water main with a pair of man-boots and twinkly earrings. She arrived on-scene, where Zack had both hands down in a hole as he spoke to another man, who was on the phone.

"Where should I be?" She kicked off her sandals and shoved her feet into her boots. Her patriotic tank top might be a casualty of the day in just a few minutes, but Rae would do whatever it took to make the facility baseball-worthy. She always did.

"I've sent Burke to turn off the water to the whole place," Zack said. As he finished speaking, the geyser in the nearby field lessened until it was gone.

"How long will it be out?" Rae glanced toward the street as if a long line of cars had piled up to enter the Sports Complex. Everything looked calm and serene—for now. In thirty minutes, the 5K would start, and runners would flood the streets, including this one. A water station was supposed to be situated here. How could they do that without water in the park?

Anxiety built in Rae's chest, pressed against her lungs until she couldn't breathe.

Zack stood, his hands dripping with mud. "Until it's fixed."

"They're going to have to excavate," she said. "We can't use this field." She took a few steps toward where the geyser had been. Water seeped up from the grass and over the toes of her boots. She was exceedingly glad in that moment that she'd kicked off her fire-engine-red sandals.

She detoured toward the next field to check the saturation level of it. Thankfully, it wasn't flooded, and she could redo the brackets to accommodate the final rounds of the tournament. She could.

"They won't excavate," Zack said. "I told them they couldn't. They're bringing the camera, and when they find the problem, they'll only dig in that one area."

Rae's annoyance seemed to shoot into the sky the same way the water had. "They're still going to dig up the field. I'll go grab the bracket and re-do it."

"You don't need to do that. The tournament doesn't start for another three hours. This will be history by then."

"Then why did you call me and tell me to get over here with my boots?"

Zack's expression stormed, and Rae stalked toward her sandals and picked them up. "You don't need me here. My whole crew will be here in ten minutes, and you've already got Burke and maintenance on the case." She started to walk away, but Zack grabbed onto her arm.

"Rae."

She pulled her arm away, sensing something bigger at play here. She didn't know what, but she didn't like the vibe Zack was putting off. "I'm going to go help April, like I was assigned to do." Her heart jumped and punched against her ribcage during the walk back to her car. Once inside, she sighed out her frustrations. She hadn't said anything to him about Ben, but she probably should have.

"Be direct," she told herself. If there was something she should've learned from her near-illegal relationship with Damian, it should've been that. "Be direct." She pulled out her phone and said, "Call Zackary McCoy," as she backed out of the small dirt lot next to the shed.

"Rae," he clipped out.

"Zack," she said in an equally business-like tone. "I don't know what's going on with you, but I'm just going to say what's on my mind. We are not together, and we are not going to get back together. I'd like to still be your friend, and you're my boss, so I'll do what I'm asked. But I did *not* need to come over here this morning, and you wasted my time."

Silence prevailed, and Rae just let it go on and on. Zack always needed several seconds to organize his thoughts. "You're right," he said. "It won't happen again. Sorry, Rae." He hung up, leaving her wondering which part she was right about. She tossed her phone onto the passenger seat, thinking *It doesn't matter. He knows we're not getting back together.*

Rae felt like a weight had been lifted from her shoulders, and she stepped into the staffing hole at the race registration with a smile on her face and her red sandals back on her feet.

———

NOT GOING TO MAKE IT TO THE PARADE. SORRY. SHE SENT HER TEXT to Ben, picked up a sandwich at a drive-through, and headed back over to the Sports Complex. Burke had texted to say that the leak had been found and the hole was being dug, but they still needed her at the complex.

Burke.

Rae had been rationalizing that texts from Burke were normal. Commonplace. They communicated all the time. But never when Zack was on-site. Never when there was such a huge problem as a broken water pipe.

She arrived back at the complex only forty-five minutes before the first game was supposed to start. The fields were full of men and women in local business T-shirts, tossing balls and getting warmed up. Two teams had taken up residence in the large soccer field just north of the ball fields as they waited for their field to be prepped.

Signs had been posted about the water, and thankfully, the people who'd brought their kids to the playground while spouses warmed up seemed understanding. Still, time gnawed at Rae's patience. Frustration boiled just beneath her skin, because she couldn't really do anything.

"How's it going?" she asked Burke from the sidewalk. No less than five city maintenance workers had gathered about center-field, and they all seemed to be wearing suits of mud.

"I heard Ozzy say they had it about ten minutes ago. He wanted to wait fifteen minutes for it to cure and then turn the water on to test."

"And Zack set up the pump?"

"My idea." Burke bumped her with his shoulder. "We still had that old machine in the back of the shed from when we drained the pond."

Rae nodded, her stomach settling enough to open her sandwich and take a bite from one of the halves. She offered the other piece to Burke, who took it with a quick, "Thanks, Rae."

Five minutes seemed to take five hours, and Ozzy—a dark-haired man in his fifties—gave a signal to someone. Rae took a breath and held it.

Second by second without water lifted Rae's spirits. Finally, someone yelled from the building near the playground, where the water main was located.

Ozzy turned toward where Rae and Burke stood and gave them a thumbs-up. Relief like Rae had never known sighed through her.

She pulled out her phone to check the time. Ben hadn't returned her text either, but maybe she could make it over to the parade in time. It had only started twenty minutes ago. She might still get to catch the part of the parade where the grocery store threw out their doughnut coupons.

Her hopes for sugar were dashed when Burke said, "C'mon, boss. They're an hour behind on concessions."

"Great," Rae said in a falsely bright voice, tucking her phone in her back pocket. Just what she needed to make her day better —nacho cheese. And maybe one of those three-foot licorice ropes. Her mouth watered as she walked with Burke over to the concession stands clustered in the middle hub of the five baseball fields.

19

Ben flipped his phone over and over during the parade. He hadn't been to an Independence Day parade in a long time. Last year, they'd been packing and gearing up to move from Oklahoma to Vermont. None of his brothers generally felt very patriotic, though their mother had made a new wreath every year for the Fourth.

As floats and police motorcycle troops went by, Ben's blood seethed. Rae should be here. She said she'd meet him here. And all she'd texted was she wasn't going to make it.

He'd wondered why for approximately two seconds. But he knew.

Work.

With Rae, it always came down to work.

Over the course of the last month, she'd clocked at least eighty hours at the rec center or Sports Complex, with Zack and Burke and dozens of other men. Ben had found a way to deal with his jealousy, and it required a lot of hours in the saddle and an equal number on his knees.

And kissing Rae whenever he could. He got a couple of hours with her on Saturday evenings, after all the soccer games, and he usually had to drag her from her office to take her to dinner or pick up pizza and go back to her place for dinner and kissing.

They had Sundays together too, and this past weekend, he'd suggested they take their own picnic into the woods, simply so he could have her to himself a little longer than he normally did. Because eight hours a week with Rae wasn't enough. Didn't satisfy.

As the days turned into weeks and then a month, Ben's desire to be a better boyfriend seemed thwarted on every side by none other than Rae herself. He'd only driven to town once during the week, picked up pizza and her favorite soda, only to eat it by himself while he waited for her to come home from the Sports Complex.

Well, he wasn't entirely alone. Beauty and Peaches kept a vigil at his feet while he ate half a pizza by himself. He hadn't tried to go into town during the week again. Even on Saturdays, he waited until she texted to say she was leaving work. Then he gave himself another thirty minutes before leaving the farm.

"You gonna text her back?" Sam finally asked, his eyes on the parade. Really, his eyes were everywhere, and Ben wondered who would call Logan on his antics once Sam went back home. Wondered who would tell him to go ride his horse when he was stressed and trying to hide it.

Ben pulled in a breath and set his phone deliberately in the mesh cup holder on his camp chair. "No."

"No?" Sam swung his gaze toward Ben. "Why not?"

Ben glared at Sam. "Maybe when you ask out Bonnie Sherman, I'll text Rae."

Sam's eyes widened and he blinked. "Bonnie Sherman?"

"I see you talk to her every Sunday. For a long time. Make Darren and Logan wait and everything."

Sam looked away, his neck turning a dark shade of red. "Don't be ridiculous."

"It's what I do best." Ben laughed and picked up his phone.

"Like right now. She just texted to say she won't make it, and I'm... bugged." He nodded and met Sam's eye. "Yeah, bugged. She said she'd be here, and she's not going to be here."

"Did she say why?"

"I know why. She's working."

Sam nodded. "She has a busy job."

"She chooses to be busier than she needs to be." Ben couldn't believe the words had come from his mouth. But they had. And he believed them to be true. "Do you think she's a little bit of a...workaholic?"

The pastor's words from weeks ago still circled in Ben's head. "Like maybe she uses work as an excuse to keep people at arm's length?"

Sam took a long drink from his bottle of water. "From what I've seen, she's hardly ever an arm's length from you." A smile accompanied the statement.

"Physically," he said. "But there's more to a relationship than that."

Sam tipped his head back and laughed. Laughed, and laughed. "Thanks for letting me know, little brother."

Ben shook his head though a smile spread his lips. "I'm just saying."

"What are you saying?" Sam looked at him again, his eyes serious now.

Ben wilted under that look from his older brother. "I don't know," he mumbled the same way he had when he was eighteen and Sam had asked him if he'd passed the GED. Ben hadn't studied for it; didn't have time. Sam wore the same inquisitive look now as he had then.

"Are you going to break up with her because she works too much?"

The high school marching band stole Ben's attention and gave him an opportunity to think before he answered. "Of course not," he said when the band had gone past. But inside, he wasn't sure.

He gripped his phone and put it back in the cup holder. He couldn't make decisions when he was upset. Frustrated. Annoyed. And he was all three right now. So he left the phone alone and watched floats and cheerleading squads and horses parade by.

———

He left his phone at the farmhouse when he went out on Willow that afternoon. He did it on purpose, because he still didn't know what to say to Rae. His unrest had been building for hours, almost to the point where he couldn't ignore it any longer.

But he didn't know what to do about it. Breaking up with Rae because she worked sounded absolutely ridiculous in his mind.

"You just miss her," he told himself as Willow meandered through the trees. He didn't direct her. She knew the way to the clearing, where her favorite grass grew. He did miss Rae. He didn't think it normal for couples to only see each other on the weekend.

But what did he know about any of it really?

Nothing, that's what. He knew nothing, which only added fuel to his frustrated fire. He dismounted and let Willow wander over to her patch of grass. He settled onto the ground under his favorite tree and leaned against the trunk.

He'd lain fully on the ground by the time the sound of rustling grass met his ears. Surprised, he sat up and searched for the source of the horse-steps. His heart somersaulted when he saw the brown and white markings of Capone.

And then Rae's flowing, dark hair, the angle of her cheekbones, the hesitant smile on her mouth. He stood quickly, brushing off his jeans and wiping his suddenly-sweaty palms down his thighs.

She slid off the horse with practiced care and whispered something to Capone, who shuffled toward Willow, several paces away.

"You left your phone at the farmhouse." She settled her weight on one foot and crossed her arms. Uncrossed them. Crossed them again.

"Yeah, I needed some space to think."

"How's that going?"

"It's...going."

"You're angry with me." She wasn't asking, and Ben didn't want to deny it.

"Not angry," he said. "Frustrated."

"Sam said angry."

"Sam should keep his mouth shut." A vein of fury joined his frustration, but he couldn't train that on Rae when it was Sam who'd spoken out of turn. Ben folded his own arms and leaned away from Rae.

"A water pipe burst at the Sports Complex. That's why I couldn't come to the parade."

"That's too bad." But Ben didn't feel bad for her. *She* didn't have to go fix it. *She* probably didn't even know how. "How did you fix it?"

"Zack called maintenance."

"So you...did what?"

Rae's eyes sparked with anger, something Ben had hardly seen her wear in her expression. He had seen that jaw work before, and his heart tripped over a beat.

"I supervised."

"Sounds stressful." Ben wasn't sure why he couldn't just accept that she'd had a rough morning. Fold her into his arms. Whisper his apologies.

Maybe because that was what he'd been doing for the better part of two months now, and he was tired of being the one who conceded all the time. He wasn't sure as this was his first serious adult relationship, but he thought there should be a little bit more give and take. Both parties needed to sacrifice something.

Until now, he'd enjoyed being the one she came to when she

needed peace, quiet, rest. But it didn't feel like that anymore. It felt like he was constantly playing second fiddle to her job. Constantly being pushed to the side, waiting in the wings, until Rae decided it was his turn to get her attention.

He took a deep breath and cleared his throat. "Remember that sermon Pastor Gray gave a few weeks ago? The one about addiction?"

Rae's eyes practically shot lightning toward him. "Yes," she said in a low tone.

"I think you get a high from your work. You're addicted to it."

"That is not true."

"You like knowing everything and having your finger on every single thing at the Sports Complex. You can't give anything to anyone else, and there are plenty of people in that rec center to help." Ben sucked in a breath. "You're a workaholic."

"Ben."

He usually loved the way she said his name. He even liked it now, but he wouldn't allow himself to be swayed this time. "You worked ninety hours last week."

"It's summer," she said. "I don't work like this all the time. As soon as the soccer season ends, things calm down."

"Do they?" Ben asked. "Because you told me last week that the baseball tournament goes all the way to the end of September."

She didn't say anything, a non-verbal confirmation to what he'd said.

"Your job is never-ending," he said.

"So is yours," she shot back. "The horses and this farm need constant care. Feeding, watering, training. It's never over."

"I work from six-thirty to four at the latest. We rotate through morning and evening chores. Logan's always been a late riser. He comes to the farm at ten and works through the evening. That's what works for us."

"This is what works for me."

He took a step toward her, his arms unclenching. "It's *not* working for you," he said. "It's not working for *us*." He reached for her and drew her unyielding body into his chest. "I miss you."

Another moment passed before she relaxed into him, before her arms came around him and held him tight. "I'll leave work earlier."

Ben didn't believe her, but he wanted to. He grasped onto the hope that she would make an effort. So he said, "Thanks, Rae," and skated his lips along her neck. By the time he matched his mouth to hers, he'd released his frustration with Rae.

She let him kiss her for several minutes before saying, "So Sam mentioned something about a barbeque?"

Ben chuckled. "Just using me for my brother's grill skills. Is that it?"

Rae beamed up at him. "That's about right." She laughed, tipping her head back the way she did when she let her joy show. Ben gazed at her, wondering how deep in he was with her and if he could ever crawl out if he had to.

He hoped he wouldn't have to, but as they collected their horses and rode back to the farm, he had to squeeze tight, tight, tight to his hope so it wouldn't float into the atmosphere and disappear.

At the same time, he wanted to let go, see where things with Rae could go, and have more faith. He'd been holding so tight to so many things for so long, and Ben was tired. Holding onto his mother through his baking. Holding on to his father by letting Sam replace him. Holding onto Sam by thinking he couldn't do adult things on his own.

Maybe it's time to let go, he thought as he returned to the farm, the scent of grilling meat filling the air.

20

The next morning, Rae set an alarm on her phone for five p.m. before she even got out of bed. She was determined to leave when the alarm went off. Leave the rec center. Leave whatever work she hadn't finished. Leave town and get out to Steeple Ridge, where Ben said he'd have Capone saddled and ready to ride.

Her day started hectic when she arrived at the rec center to find emergency vehicles filling the circle drive. A firefighter had over-exerted himself on the stair climber, she discovered after making it past the yellow tape and down to her office.

She had trophies to order for the soccer teams, and seventeen team managers to call about next weekend's baseball tournament. The schedule had been posted for a few weeks, and Rae checked it to make sure the most updated version had populated correctly.

April entered her office and sat down, a thick folder on her lap. "Let's review the budget for the aquatics center. The City Council is voting on it next Tuesday."

Rae glanced up from the order forms she hadn't finished yet. "Isn't Zack presenting that?"

"He gave it to me on Monday." April glanced up and back to the folder so quickly, Rae couldn't determine how she felt about having the presentation given to her so late in the game. "Apparently he's taking a few weeks of leave this month."

Rae's eyebrows practically shot off her forehead. "He's what?"

The high-pitched nature of Rae's voice caused April to abandon her examination of the top paper in the folder. "He's taking three weeks of personal leave. Starting on Monday." She frowned and twirled a lock of hair around her forefinger. "He didn't tell you?"

"He hasn't mentioned it, no." Rae glanced out the door, as if Zack would appear with an explanation. He didn't.

"I'm guessing you'll have to pick up a lot of what he usually does," April said. "He hasn't said anything?"

"We meet on Wednesdays," Rae said. "We didn't meet yesterday because of the Fourth activities." Zack hadn't rescheduled the meeting, and Rae stood. "Can you give me a sec?" She didn't wait for April to confirm before marching out of her office and across the hall to Zack's.

He sat with his back to the door, in the chair on the wrong side of his desk, his feet kicked up on the tabletop. "What do you want, Rae?" He sounded half-bored, half-annoyed. He didn't turn around to face her, which only increased her ire.

"You're taking three weeks of personal leave starting Monday?"

"Yes."

Rae's mouth opened and closed without any sound coming out, like a fish. She was finally able to articulate, "Well, when were you planning to tell me?"

Zack waved one hand in the air, still refusing to look at her. "I don't know."

Her heart banged against her ribcage. She thought about the alarm she'd set on her phone. There was no way she could do her job *and* his and leave by five each evening. Maybe if she came into work at four in the morning.

She seized onto the idea. Ben would never know....

"What do you need me to do while you're gone?" She entered the office for the first time since Ben had interrupted her and Zack and perched on the edge of his desk. She stared at him until he swung his attention toward her.

Hurt swam in his eyes, and Rae's stomach ached that she'd been the cause of it. She really wasn't interested in him, and she hadn't realized he still harbored feelings for her.

"I'll email you," he said.

"When?"

"Later."

"Zack." She inched a little closer to him. "What's going on with you?"

"I just need...a break. I'm starting to hate the job, you know? And I've never hated the job."

Rae knew the feeling, though she hadn't realized her dislike for the job until it threatened her relationship with Ben. "Are you leaving town?"

"Probably."

"Probably?" Rae couldn't believe his casualness about this leave of absence. "You haven't decided?"

"No, Rae." His words held a bit of snap. "I haven't decided."

"Where will you go?"

"Maybe Nova Scotia. I hear it's nice in the summer. Cooler. Ocean-y." His slate gray eyes found hers and pierced right through her soul. Back when they were dating, she'd told him she wanted to go to Nova Scotia in the summer. Visit the ocean and dip her toes in the cooler water.

She swallowed and shored up her courage. "That sounds nice." She straightened and headed for the door before he could see her emotion. "I'll watch for your email."

Zack didn't respond as she left. She settled behind her desk again and faced April, who wore concern in her eyes. "Everything okay?"

Rae shook her head, her chest a storm of emotions. She didn't mean to hurt Zack. He'd never hated the job—until he couldn't have her? Why now? They'd dated a long time ago, and she'd dated plenty of people in between him and Ben.

She couldn't worry about Zack, not with the thick folder still perched in her assistant's lap. "April, I'm going to need your help to make it through the month."

April edged forward on her seat and set the folder on Rae's desk. "Of course."

"Can you go grab Meredith? I want to pow-wow."

April got up and left without another word, and Rae's friends returned only half a minute later. "What's going on?" Meredith came around the desk and stared down at Rae. "Why do you look like you lost Ralph again?"

"Zack's taking a three-week personal leave," April said as she took the chair.

"And Ben thinks I'm a workaholic," Rae said, which really sent a charge into the silence. "I promised him I'd leave work by five on weekdays. Make more time for us to be together."

Meredith started nodding before Rae stopped speaking. "You like him." She wasn't asking.

Rae couldn't help smiling or nodding. "I like him. And I do work a lot."

"Only in the summer," Meredith said.

But Rae shook her head, the truth infiltrating her system the way her blood did. "No, I think Ben's right. It's always something with me. There's always something here. I work ten to twelve hours a day no matter what time of year it is. I'm always here on Saturday, even if it's just a few hours."

She glanced from April to Meredith. "I don't want to lose him." She didn't say what she really felt: She was falling in love with him. Thought he might be the one who could love her back despite her flaws. But not if she never saw him, never made time for him.

"All right." Meredith marched out of the room and returned with the chair from Zack's office. "Let's get you out of here by five o'clock." She nodded once like that was that.

A rush of gratitude flowed through Rae, and she sent a prayer toward heaven that she could satisfy Ben *and* get the job done at the rec center.

———

RAE MET HER GOAL ON THURSDAY AND FRIDAY. SATURDAY, SHE PUT in her time at the morning soccer games and sat next to Ben on the grass at the Sports Complex as fireworks lit the night sky. She'd gone into her office for a couple of hours after the games, because Zack had finally deemed it necessary to send her a list of what she needed to do in his absence. She'd organized his notes and made a list for Monday morning before rushing out to the farm to pick up Ben for dinner.

They'd spent a great evening together, and Rae had definitely enjoyed the downtime. She actually felt jealous of Zack's personal leave and wished she could take the next three weeks off to really explore how she felt about Ben. As it was, she had to compartmentalize everything. Work now. Think about Ben later.

Work all day. Talk to Ben in the evening.

Work, work, work. Ben, Ben, Ben.

Over the course of the next two weeks, Rae felt like she was constantly juggling. She woke exhausted. Worked like a dog, eating on the go or not at all. Tried to be a better girlfriend with the little remaining energy she had. Collapsed in bed as soon as she got home from the farm or from dinner out, or she fell asleep on her couch if Ben came to her place.

She left work at five every evening except Thursdays, when the Sports Complex hosted youth soccer games. She only went to the fields for the Saturday morning games, never to the office afterward.

With only two weeks until the soccer season ended, Rae's workload increased. She had scores to tally, and championship brackets to make, and coaches' meetings to plan and execute. There was no way she could keep up with the physical maintenance of the Sports Complex and all the paperwork on the business side and be done by five o'clock.

So Rae did what she'd thought of weeks ago. She got up earlier. Went into the rec center by seven instead of nine. Ben didn't need to know. Soccer season would end in two weeks, and Zack would return in one, and Rae could survive with only six hours of sleep for a couple of weeks. She could.

She started praying on the way to work each morning. Praying for strength and stamina. Praying that she could persevere. She did feel like something divine was buoying her up, helping her through the hours that seemed to pass in a single breath, with little work accomplished.

She didn't leave work on time on Monday, but it wasn't her fault. Burke had called in sick, and Rae had gone to check with her crew at the Sports Complex. Thankfully, she hadn't planned anything with Ben and was able to pick up a pizza on her way home and be in bed by eight-thirty, mere minutes after eating.

By mid-afternoon on Tuesday, she knew she wasn't going to make it out to the farm for riding and resting in the shaded forest. She texted Ben to tell him, and he came back with, *No problem. Want me to bring you dinner?*

She did, but she didn't want him to see the state of her office or how frazzled and tired she looked. *No, April's ordering from the diner*, she messaged. Then she texted April to ask her to order dinner from the diner that evening, as they'd be in her office organizing the flag football teams until the job was finished.

Wednesday, she met with the aquatic center's architect, which took the entire morning. Calls and emails about the final week of soccer took her afternoon, and she hadn't even gotten to the basketball registrations Zack normally handled.

She stood in her office, her breath coming in quick bursts. She hadn't had a panic attack before, but if she had to guess, she was having one right now. The world thinned to just her desk, with whiteness blanketing everything else.

Her breath wheezed, the sound of it as loud as a tornado, rushing and racing through her ears. She pressed one hand against her chest and the other against her desk.

The episode passed as quickly as it had started, leaving her sweaty and lightheaded. She made it to her desk chair and sank into it, utterly spent.

"I can't do this," she whispered. Her eyes couldn't seem to focus on any one thing, and she leaned her head back against the chair. She needed to call Ben.

She didn't know why, or what she would say, but she needed to call Ben. She didn't. Rae tried to focus on the multiple piles in front of her, but the mounds of paper suffocated her. She leapt from her desk and strode out of her office. When she hit the hall, she started running.

She drove fifteen over the speed limit on her way to Steeple Ridge, her heart bobbing in the back of her throat the whole way. Words didn't form in her mind or mouth. She just needed to see Ben. He'd calm her down. He'd fix what had broken inside her.

She pulled into the parking lot with a cloud of dust and searched for Ben. She had no idea where he'd be at just after noon, so she headed toward the farmhouse. No one was inside, and Rae took a moment to enjoy the silence and the scent of something masculine.

"Rae?"

She turned to find Ben standing in the doorway, dusting his hands against each other. She didn't speak, just flew toward him.

He caught her with a grunt and asked, "What are you doing here?"

"I can't do this," she said, gulping for air. "I'm drowning."

He stroked her hair. "Hey, calm down. Tell me what's going on."

She stepped back. Stepped away completely. "I can't—" She swallowed, hard. "I can't be the girlfriend you deserve. I'm sorry." She started past him, and he swung his head around as she walked out the back door.

"Rae," he said. "Wait a minute."

She paused next to the picnic table they'd sat on a few times over the past couple of weeks. He'd held her hand there, and everything in her life had seemed to move so slowly. At the same time she'd enjoyed it, she'd catalogued all the time she was losing on her projects at work.

Ben positioned himself between her and the parking lot. "I think you're doing a great job at being my girlfriend."

Her desperation welled in her throat, unclogging when she shook her head. "I've been going to work two hours early so I can still leave on time. I'm exhausted all the time. I never take a lunch." Tears gathered in her eyes. "I can't keep doing this. I'm doing a shoddy job at work. I feel guilty when I'm with you. I feel guilty when I'm not with you." She looked over his shoulder, trying to dismiss the next words that entered her mind.

They wouldn't be dismissed. Or contained. "I'm sorry, Ben." Her voice broke on his name. "But I can't be with you right now." She strode away from him, breaking into a run when he called her name.

She didn't go back to her office, despite the mountains of work waiting for her there. She didn't go home, as Ben would likely look there for her. She simply checked the level of fuel in her gas tank and set her car on the two-lane highway leading out of town.

21

Numbness had descended on Ben as soon as Rae had torn out of the parking lot at Steeple Ridge. He wasn't entirely sure how long he stood in the shadows of the farmhouse before heading back to the barn, where he'd been working when Rae had shown up unannounced.

His hands lifted bales of hay. Moved horses from one stall to another to clean. His legs carried him up the aisle and back down. To the wash stalls and back. Out to the pastures and back to the barn.

He didn't see Sam or Logan or Darren, and he didn't expect to. The twins were out in the fields, and Sam was in the office making travel plans for his trip to Wyoming.

Ben seized onto the thought of Wyoming and abandoned his job in the barn without a backward glance. "Sam," he called as he entered the house. He leaned in the doorway of the office, slightly out of breath. "Can I come to Wyoming with you?"

Sam blinked and frowned, frowned and blinked some more. "I'm just going for a few days. Getting house care lined up again. Visiting the graves." He stood and leaned his weight into his palms on the desk. "You said you didn't want to go."

"I changed my mind." Ben lifted his chin, almost daring Sam to question him further. Which, of course he would.

Sam sighed. "I'm not moving until next spring, Ben. We've been—"

"This isn't about that," Ben said. Over the past couple of weeks, he'd talked a lot to Sam about all the things he'd been clutching tightly in his fist, including the memories of his parents and his idolization of Sam.

Ben felt like he'd been making great strides forward. In life. In his job responsibilities. In his relationship with Rae. Sure, he'd noticed how tired she was. Sometimes she acted a bit distant, checked out. But she was *trying*, and that was what mattered to him. She was *trying* to make time for him.

He'd been trying to give her a soft spot to land. A quiet place within the circle of his arms to just be herself. A calm inside the storm of her insanely busy job.

He thought he'd been doing pretty well. He didn't understand what had just happened.

"Rae broke up with me," he blurted. "I want to go to Wyoming with you." He couldn't stand to be this close to Rae and not be able to stop by her house and kiss her just because he felt like it.

"Rae broke up with you?" Sam glanced over Ben's shoulder as if a witness would come forward and corroborate the story. "Why?"

Ben's chest quaked with every breath. Why did air seem like the wrong thing to breathe? Was this how drowning felt?

I'm drowning.

Rae had said that. *I'm drowning.*

And it was his fault. He suddenly knew exactly why she'd broken up with him. "I put too much pressure on her to leave work at a decent hour."

Sam picked up his cowboy hat and smashed it on his head. "Let's go ride."

"I don't want to ride." And Ben didn't. He rarely disagreed

with Sam, but he once again lifted his chin. "Can I book a ticket to Wyoming? What time is your flight?" He moved toward the laptop on the desk. Sam stepped out of the way, a wary, sympathetic edge in his eyes that Ben didn't understand. But he didn't worry about it either. He was an adult, and if he wanted to go to Wyoming with his brother, he was going to go.

———

Four days later, Ben and Sam touched down in Billings. Getting on an airplane and flying had been much easier this time, and Ben went through the line to get the rental car while Sam found something to eat.

"Did you tell Rae you were leaving town?" He handed Ben a brown paper bag and a soda cup.

Ben sucked on the straw and shook his head. "They gave us a sedan this time."

"There's just two of us," Sam said around a mouthful of chicken sandwich. "Should be fine."

"Did you tell Bonnie you were coming to Wyoming?" Ben started toward the parking lot, checking the stall number he'd been given.

"No." Sam gave him a look that didn't do anything to warn Ben away. "I'm not dating her. I'm not in love with her."

Ben scoffed, the sound morphing into a full-blown laugh. "I'm not dating Rae either. And I'm certainly not in love with her." The words slid easily out of his throat, though he did question their validity. For the month of July, he'd thought every day with Rae was pure perfection. He thought sure this was what love felt like. But he'd never been in love, and he wasn't sure. He'd needed more time, and he'd told himself to be patient, to wait and see how life with Rae was in the fall. The winter. The spring. Then he'd know if he could endure another summer season with her working more than any human should have to work.

Sam let Ben's statement slide. But Ben pressed the Bonnie issue with, "You took her to dinner last week."

"No," Sam said in a tone he reserved for Logan when he was horsing around. "I ran into her at the coffee shop."

"Then you walked across the street and got a doughnut to go with it." Ben raised his eyebrows. "You sat at a table together and talked. With food in front of you. That's called a date."

Sam rolled his eyes and adjusted the air conditioning in the rental car. "Yeah, since you know *so* much about dating."

A knife stabbed into Ben's chest, making a wounded sound slip from his mouth.

"Sorry, Ben," Sam said quickly. "I didn't mean that."

Ben shook his head. "It's fine." But nothing inside him felt fine. His internal organs felt like someone had removed them from his body and stuffed them back in in the wrong places.

Sam let several miles go by in silence. Then he said, "What are you going to do about Rae?"

"Nothing to be done." Ben reached for the radio and turned up the volume.

Sam turned it down. "Have you called her?"

"No," he said, glancing at Sam. "Why would I call her? What would I even say?"

Sam shrugged and looked out his window. "I don't know."

Ben chuckled, the mood lightening. "Yeah, that's why you *went out* with Bonnie over two weeks ago and haven't talked to her since."

"I've talked to her since then."

"When?" Ben challenged. "You practically ran from the chapel last week."

"I'm moving to Wyoming in eight months. I'm in no position to start dating a woman who lives in Vermont."

"Maybe Bonnie would move to Wyoming with you."

Sam started laughing, and he didn't stop for several seconds.

He looked at Ben, took a breath, and laughed again. "We're both hopeless with women," he said.

Ben flexed his fingers on the steering wheel and didn't argue. He'd been trying to rely more on his faith and less on gripping things he couldn't let go of. He hadn't baked pretzels in weeks, and he didn't miss his mother any more or any less. He'd been taking on more adult responsibilities like buying more dish-washing liquid before they ran out.

The edge of Coral Canyon appeared on the horizon, and Ben's heart twisted. The anniversary of his parents' deaths was only in two days, and the hole in his chest expanded. Maybe he did miss his mother more than he'd admitted, soft pretzels or no soft pretzels.

Ben hated that his efforts to overcome some of his inadequacies had amounted to very little. He wanted to call Rae and talk to her about his parents. He wanted to lie under the trees and hold her hand on the anniversary of their deaths.

She hadn't called him, but that didn't mean he had to stay silent too. He reached for his phone. "Do you mind if I call Rae?"

"Right now?" Sam turned off the radio completely. "What are you going to say?"

Nerves danced through him as he grinned at his brother and dialed Rae. "I have no idea."

Her phone rang and rang and rang. He wasn't sure if it was because she was too busy working—or because she didn't want to talk specifically to him.

Doesn't matter, he told himself as the call went to her voice-mail. He almost hung up, but at the sound of her voice saying, "Hey, it's Rae. Talk to me," everything inside him softened.

"Hey, Rae," he said. "It's Ben. I'm in Wyoming for a few days, and I...." He glanced at Sam, who watched him like he was the most interesting show on the planet. "I'm thinking about you. Maybe you could call me later." He inhaled, exhaled. "Okay, bye."

He hung up and set the phone in the console. "She didn't answer."

Sam nodded and reached over to pat Ben's arm. The comfort between them seemed bottomless. Ben enjoyed the silence, the peace that existed in the small town of Coral Canyon, and the sight of his childhood home as he pulled into the driveway. He and Sam sat in the car for a few seconds before they looked at each other.

"I like it here," Ben said. "It feels like home."

Sam gave him a joyful smile. "It sure does."

Over the next couple of days, Ben cleaned up the yard while Sam found someone in town to take care of the house for the next eight months.

The anniversary of his parents' deaths dawned early, and warm, and bright. The sky didn't hold a single cloud as Ben clipped a handful of the pink lemonade roses his mother had carefully tended to. He tied the stems together with a piece of white string he found in the kitchen and joined Sam on the front steps.

"Ready?" Sam asked.

"Not really." Ben played with the ends of the string. "But yeah. I'm ready." He stood and headed around to the back yard. It had never felt like such a long walk before, but today it did. He and Sam finally reached the edge of the yard, where a fence separated the lawn from the fields.

Two headstones sat there, and Ben crouched down and swept his hand across the letters of his mother's name. The stone felt cool in the morning air, and gritty from the dirt and dust.

"Hey, Mom." He laid the flowers at the base of the grave marker and stood, tucking his hands in his pockets. Sam laid the flowers he'd cut on his father's grave.

"Love you, Dad." Ben swallowed, trying to keep his emotion contained deep down inside his chest. When Sam swiped his hand across his eyes, Ben gave in to the urge to cry. A single tear slid down his face, and he wiped it away silently.

He took a very slow breath and closed his eyes. "Can I say a prayer?"

Sam sniffed and nodded.

Ben wasn't sure what to say, but the words came easily. By the end of the short plea for comfort, a sense of peace had settled on him. He reached for Sam, and put his arm around his brother's shoulders.

"Thanks for taking care of me," he said.

"Sometimes you took care of me," Sam said.

Ben looked at him. "When?"

Sam gave half a shrug. "There were some times I didn't think I could keep going, and then you'd come into my bedroom late at night, and I knew I had to. God helped in the hardest times." He glanced at Ben. "We have a lot to be grateful for."

Ben nodded and focused back on the graves. "We sure do."

They stood in silence for several minutes. Sam finally sighed and said, "I'm gonna head back to the house."

"All right. I'm gonna stay a while longer."

Sam walked away, and Ben sat down on the grass, threading several blades through his fingers. "Mom," he said. "I was dating this woman in Island Park. She was nice. I mean, she *is* nice. And smart. And beautiful." A smile played across his face. "She loves soft pretzels."

He stopped talking, not really sure why he was telling his mother about Rae. He let his thoughts wander, and he told his parents about Steeple Ridge, and his horse, and the dog that Logan loved but everyone else could barely tolerate.

He fell silent again, and the sun began to become too warm to be comfortable.

"Mom, how do you know when you're in love with someone?"

Of course his mom didn't answer. A breeze kicked up, and

Ben listened carefully for something higher than himself. Something to guide him. Anything.

"Do I love Rae?" he asked, wondering if the Lord could even tell him such things. He wasn't sure how it happened, but it felt like he'd uncurled his fist and let go of his need to know how he felt.

And then he suddenly knew.

His eyes popped open. "I'm in love with her."

"Duh," Sam said, causing Ben to twist around.

"How long have you been standing there?"

"Couple of minutes." He sat beside Ben. "I just came to check on you. You've been out here a long time."

"Just thinking."

Sam nudged his shoulder. "And talking out loud to yourself."

Ben grinned. "Family habit."

"Whatever. I don't do that."

"Mom did."

"Yeah." Sam glanced at the headstone. "She did." He took a big breath and focused on Ben again. "So you're in love with Rae?"

Fear sliced right through Ben. "Yeah." He looked at Sam, all his fear and anxiety laid open. "What am I going to do now?"

Sam chuckled. "You're asking me? I can't even ask out the woman I like."

"Ha!" Ben shoved Sam's shoulder. "I knew you liked Bonnie."

Sam swatted at him. "Of course I like her. But she has...issues."

Ben laughed. Laid back in the grass and laughed. "Have you met my girlfriend? She works a million hours a week. She *wants* to work a million hours a week. Talk about issues."

Sam stood and offered his hand to Ben. "No, I think she wants you."

Ben took his brother's hand and got to his feet. "What makes you think that?"

"She tried, Ben." They started walking back toward the house. "She left work at five o'clock. Came out to the farm to spend time with you. She *tried*."

Happiness spread through Ben but it only stayed for a few seconds. "She hasn't called me back."

"You'll figure out what to do," Sam said.

Ben's chest swelled, because for maybe the first time, he felt mature enough and grounded enough to find his own way.

His own way back to Rae.

22

R ae didn't need to call her voicemail to hear Ben's message. She had it memorized. Still, she dialed in just to hear him say "Hey, Rae," in that throaty, playful voice he used when he was about to kiss her.

Hey, Rae.

It's Ben. I'm in Wyoming for a few days, and I...I'm thinking about you. Maybe you could call me later.

Pause.

Okay, bye.

She hadn't called him back. She wasn't sure why. Probably because for the past several days she hadn't been the walking dead. Her stomach hadn't been sour with guilt layered upon guilt, and she'd been able to sleep deeply for the first time in weeks.

Something nagged at her conscience. She couldn't settle into a task at work. She kept telling herself it was because Zack was supposed to stop by that afternoon, get briefed on everything that had happened while he'd been gone.

But she knew that wasn't it.

Finally, after a couple of hours of shuffling papers around,

Rae got up and closed her office door. She returned to her desk
and sat down, inhaling a slow, deliberate breath. She'd been prac-
ticing a few meditation strategies since her flight from Island
Park. From Ben.

The day she'd ended things with him, she'd stayed the night
in Burlington, then risen early and driven straight back to work.
Wore the same clothes and everything. She'd been existing in
straight lines for the past four days. Drive to the rec center. Drive
home. Rec center. Home.

She didn't even allow herself to deviate to the Sports
Complex, which would take her down the road that led out to
Steeple Ridge. And she didn't trust herself not to head straight
out there and beg Ben to take her back.

Feeling centered, she bowed her head and prayed. *Dear Lord.
What should I be doing?*

Her prayers usually went on much longer as she pleaded with
God to direct her, to provide for her what she so sorely needed.
The problem was, Rae didn't really know *what* she needed. In the
past, her wants and needs hadn't aligned, and she had no reason
to think they were in harmony this time either.

And so her prayers had simplified. She'd almost given up
control to the Lord. As she released the last bit of hold she had, a
sense of freedom penetrated her thoughts so strongly, she started
weep.

She didn't hear a voice. A light didn't shine down from
heaven. Rae simply knew that God was there and that He loved
her, workaholic tendencies and all.

After several seconds, Rae wiped her face and took another
deliberate breath.

"Now what?" she wondered as the same creeping feeling that
she needed to do something returned.

Like lightning arcing from the sky, a thought struck her. God
loved her, yes. But if she wanted Ben to love her, she might need
to change.

You should call him back, she thought.

She reached for her phone without hesitation.

Her heart galloped around her chest like a herd of wild horses. She found Ben's name in her contacts easily, but she couldn't press send. Instead, she dialed her mom.

"Mom," she said. "Can you meet for lunch today?"

"Sure, baby. The diner?"

"I'm feeling like a big old bowl of pasta," Rae said. "Can we meet at La Ferrovia in a couple of hours?"

"Pasta? What's going on?"

Rae closed her eyes and said, "I broke up with Ben." Her mom was going to find out anyway. Rae was actually surprised she didn't already know.

"Oh."

That was all. No more questions. No advice. Just "oh."

"Twelve-thirty?" Rae asked, a slight tremor in her voice.

"See you then, sweetheart."

Rae ended the call and stared at the wall across from her desk. She'd mounted her diploma there, flanked by two photographs an old high school friend had taken of the sunrise and sunset in Island Park.

Her phone chimed a calendar reminder, pulling Rae back to her tasks. Instead of sighing and picking up another folder or returning to the flyer she'd been creating for an upcoming babysitting training class, she shot to her feet. Grabbed her phone. And headed out.

"I'll be back in a few hours," she told Meredith as she passed.

"Okay. Hey." She stood and came around the desk, catching Rae's arm to stop her from running off. "What's going on?"

"Nothing. I just have some stuff to do." It wasn't exactly a lie.

"You have that look in your eye."

"What look?"

"This wild look." Meredith stepped back and wrung her hands. "I'm worried about you. You don't look as tired as you have the past couple of weeks, but this...this is something even worse."

A small fire started in Rae's blood. "Mer, I'm fine."

"You broke up with Ben. You're not fine."

Rae glanced around as if the paparazzi cared about her country relationship with Ben Buttars. "I just need to get through this month and next month," she said. "Then I'll call him."

"You think he's going to wait for two months?" Meredith scoffed even as her cheeks blushed. "I don't want to upset you, and I do just want you to be happy. But say he does take you back in two months. What about next summer?"

Rae shook her head. She couldn't even think about that afternoon. No way she could start worrying about next summer. "I have to go." She turned and hurried toward the doors.

"When are you going to admit you're in love with him?"

Rae ignored Meredith and pushed into the summer sunshine. She donned her sunglasses so the patrons entering the rec center couldn't read the panic in her eyes and half-jogged, half-walked to her car.

She sat behind the wheel, her thoughts tumbling, rumbling, mumbling through her mind. She gripped the wheel, her indecision almost like a scent on the air.

"I need to do something hard," she said. "Help me to do something hard."

She put the car in gear and headed home, her nerves so close to the surface she couldn't contain them beneath her skin. A sob escaped her mouth when she pulled into the driveway, and she bypassed her pets and went straight down the hall to her bedroom.

She locked the door though she didn't expect anyone to come in. After all, Ben was in Wyoming, and her mother would work until twelve-twenty-nine and then hurry down the street to the Italian restaurant.

Pressing her back against the door, she practiced her deep

breathing and managed to calm the tears. Then she walked with sure steps to her closet and positioned the footstool she used to reach way back on the top shelf.

She climbed up and pushed aside a couple of sweatshirts she hadn't worn in months. The hard edge of the shoebox met her fingers, and she scrabbled to get a grip on it. She finally did and pulled it free. Holding it with two hands, she took it with her into the bedroom and sat on the end of her bed.

The top of the box came off easily, and the medals inside didn't glimmer the way they did when she'd first won them. Time and dust and neglect had taken their toll, and Rae reached with hesitant fingers to touch them.

The metal held a chill and the texture of dust coated her skin. "I used to love horseback riding," she said to her empty house. She'd given it up because of a single comment from a man who meant nothing to her.

She glanced up. Would she give up Ben as easily?

That intense pressure band around her chest returned, and she exhaled. She shook her head. "No." She glanced toward the door as if Ben would walk through it. He sure didn't, but Rae hoped that someday he would. Someday soon.

Decision made, Rae sprang to her feet. She checked her watch. She had time. Time to get back to the rec center and take care of something before she met her mom for lunch.

————

RAE STOOD WHEN HER MOM WALKED INTO THE RESTAURANT, TEN minutes late. "Hey, Mom." She gave her mom a strong hug and added, "I already ordered for you. Eggplant parmesan with fettuccine Alfredo."

"My favorite." Her mom grinned and slid into the chair across from Rae. "Sorry I'm late. Right when I was leaving, a big group of teens came into the drug store."

"Oh yeah? Loading up on penny candy?"

"Yes!" Her mom rolled her eyes. "I know they're putting in more than they say, but I am not counting out one hundred Swedish fish."

Rae smiled at her mom and leaned her elbows on the table. "Mom, I have something exciting to tell you."

Her curiosity piqued, her mom finally stopped fiddling with her phone and her purse and her drug store uniform. She stared at Rae and lifted her left eyebrow in the way Rae loved. "Do tell."

Rae heaved the box of medals onto the table. "First, tell me what you can remember about these."

Her mom leaned forward and peered into the box. "Your show medals?" She lifted the top one out of the box. "You won this one in jumping." She gazed at the medal with affection. "You loved jumping. You were so good at it." Her mom glanced up, but not long enough to truly make eye contact. "And you and Evita were so good together." She slid the box closer and pulled out another medal, this one just as gold as the first. "This was for dressage."

Rae let her mom go through the medals, because it made her teenage memories of her horse showing days more vibrant. She'd put them on the shelf with her medals, and they were just as dusty as the physical objects her mom pulled out one by one.

The food arrived and Rae took the medals back so she could dig into her half-and-half spaghetti special. She tore off a chunk of bread and wiped it through the spot where the marinara sauce met the Alfredo sauce.

"So what were you going to tell me?" her mom asked.

The realization Rae had had in her bedroom, clutching the box of medals to her chest, suddenly dammed up against the back of her throat. The same warmth cascaded over her skin now as it had then.

"I'm in love with Ben Buttars, and I quit my job an hour ago."

———

AFTER REASSURING HER MOTHER THAT SHE WAS NOT INSANE, THAT she had indeed thought things through, and eaten all of her spaghetti and meatballs, she drove out to Steeple Ridge. She knew Ben wasn't there, but she'd called him three times without getting an answer. Her stomach writhed and her skin felt like someone had poured liquid glue all over her and let it dry.

She scratched her arm but couldn't find relief. She pulled onto the road that led to the farmhouse and parked near the front lawn the way Ben did. In the middle of the afternoon, she didn't know who she expected to see.

She got out of the car and stretched, the sky above her clear and wonderful. The smell at Steeple Ridge was different from everywhere else, and there was something special about it Rae couldn't put her finger on.

Turning back to the house, she heard, "Rae. What are you doing here?"

Darren stood at the corner of the house, his hands hanging at his side. Logan joined him a few seconds later. Tension drifted toward her, and she didn't like the taste of it.

She crossed the lawn, expecting Logan to crack a joke or at least smile. He simply watched her. Darren was the serious twin, with the driest sense of humor on the planet. Rae normally enjoyed trying to get him to smile, relished the one time she'd gotten him to laugh at something she'd said at Sunday dinner.

Her eyes volleyed between the two brothers. "What's going on?"

"Nothing." Logan started toward the back yard, and Rae followed. "You know Ben's not here, right?"

"Yeah." She sat on the bench at the end of the picnic table while the brothers climbed on top, the way Ben always did. "He called. But I haven't been able to get him to answer my calls today." She tired to make her voice nonchalant, but she failed completely. "Do you guys know what he might be doing in Wyoming today?"

She searched their faces, seeing every emotion from sorrow to pain to worry. "Yeah," Darren finally said. "We know what they're doin' in Wyoming today." He met Logan's eyes. Eyes she'd never seen so withdrawn, so forlorn.

"What am I missing?" she asked.

"Today's the anniversary of our parents' deaths," Darren said in an even voice. "My guess is Ben and Sam are out on the edge of the yard where we buried them. Taking it easy. They've probably gone dark. Ben especially likes to ditch his phone when he's not up to talking to anyone."

"He took our parents' deaths the hardest," Logan answered as his dog came trotting over from the pasture. Rambo sat at Logan's feet, close enough for Rae to reach out and pat, which she did. The shepherd barely gave her a glance, but tipped his head back to look at Logan. Rambo whined, and Logan gave him half a smile.

"I had no idea," Rae said. "I mean, he said they'd died in the fall, but I didn't realize it was August."

"Yeah." Darren nodded as silence fell over them.

Rae's brain—which had basically betrayed her all day—started firing again. She had nothing keeping her here. The man she loved was in Wyoming, suffering on the ten-year anniversary of his parents' death.

She stood and wiped her palms down her thighs, the ideas in her head absolutely ridiculous. "I think I better go."

"He'll call you back," Darren said as Rae opened the screen door to go through the house to the front, where she'd parked. "Give him some time, and he'll call you back."

"Thanks, Darren." Rae walked into the kitchen and paused. She took in a deep breath, trying to find the familiar and distinct scent of salt and pretzel dough. She couldn't, almost like Ben hadn't been baking lately.

Her heart cracked, and determination filled her. She should've been the one to go with Ben to visit his parents' graves. The stupid tears she hadn't been able to tame for weeks appeared instantly, and she headed toward the car, suddenly anxious to get as far from Steeple Ridge Farm as possible.

23

Ben stayed in bed long after he woke. The light was blue and gray and gold behind his closed eyes. Yesterday had drained him completely, and he was glad Sam had foreseen such an emotional investment in visiting the graves and taking care of the house.

Ideas bounced around in Ben's mind, almost as fast as pinballs ricocheting from one side of his skull to the other. When the smell of coffee met his nose, he threw off the blankets and headed into the kitchen.

Sam stood at the sink, a mug in his hand. "I'm meetin' the caretaker for lunch. You're welcome to come."

Ben poured himself a cup of coffee and dumped an obscene amount of sugar in it. "What if I move here?" he said. "I can take care of the house until you can come."

Sam turned from his position at the window, his face molded with pure surprise. "You want to move here?"

Ben couldn't see his brother's eyebrows because they stretched so high. "It's not the worst idea ever."

"Yes, Ben, it is." Sam set his mug on the counter and leaned against the sink. "Rae lives in Vermont."

"Yeah."

"Rae, *the woman you're in love with*."

Ben took a long drink of scalding coffee and immediately regretted it. "She broke up with me."

"So you're going to run away?"

The implication of his immaturity stung Ben. "I'm just saying that we need someone to take care of the house until next spring, and I'm available."

"If that's the only requirement, I could move here too."

Ben shook his head. "You have a contract to train that stallion for the richest man in New York."

Sam scoffed. "He's not the richest man in New York."

Ben chuckled, but the sound carried more darkness than happiness. "I believe those were your exact words."

"Tucker could do it."

"Tucker barely knows the difference between a horse and a cow."

Sam blinked, and then a laugh exploded out of his mouth. "That's not true. He does all right."

"Yeah, well, there's no way he can train that stallion. I've seen The Baron. He has a fiery temperament."

"I'm going to do it," Sam said, twisting back to the window. "I need the money."

"You do not. We have plenty of money." He joined his brother and looked across the back yard to where the graves were. The sun barely glinted off the tops of them. "Did you know Mom and Dad had that much money?"

Sam shook his head. "My recollection is that we never had much growing up."

"But we didn't go without."

"No, we didn't."

Enough time passed that Ben finished his coffee. Sam asked, "You don't really want to move here for the winter, do you?"

Rae's beautiful face passed through his mind. "No," he said. "I would like to go to a movie today, though."

Sam smiled, and Ben saw the youthfulness in his face when he did. "All right, we'll—"

The peal of the doorbell interrupted him, and he and Ben stared at each other. "Who could that be?" Sam asked, leaving his half-empty mug in the sink and striding toward the front door.

Ben followed, his curiosity piqued. He leaned against the wall separating the living room from the kitchen as Sam pulled open the door amidst a squeal from the hinges.

A beautiful brunette stood on the doorstep, her hair pulled back in its trademark ponytail.

"Rae?" Sam and Ben said at the same time.

Ben blinked and everything in his vision flashed to white for an extra second.

"Hey." Rae shuffled half a foot forward and fell back again. "So I stopped at the gas station on the edge of town, and a guy named George told me where you lived." She glanced to her left, down the road toward town. "I flew most of the night."

"Come in," Sam said, stepping back. He even reached for her arm as if she couldn't lift her foot the one step up into the living room.

Ben couldn't seem to move at all. His heart pranced around his chest like it had been knocked loose, and his brain had stopped functioning completely.

"Ben," Sam said. "Rae's here."

Rae's here.

Ben's heart latched itself back into place and he lurched forward before yanking his hand back. His first instinct was to sweep her off her feet and kiss her. His second was to build a wall around his still-racing heart and protect himself.

"Maybe you'd like to take her for a walk," Sam said, a heavy note of suggestion in his voice.

"Yeah." Ben's voice sounded like he'd swallowed helium. He

cleared his throat. "Yeah, sure." He hadn't looked away from Rae once. "Do you want to go for a walk?"

She nodded and tucked a non-existent piece of hair behind her ear. She let her hand fall to her side, her face holding a beautiful blush. "Sure." She moved back the way she'd come, and Ben started to follow.

"Tell her," Sam hissed out of the corner of his mouth as Ben passed. Ben swung his attention to Sam and paused.

"You think I should tell her?"

"She flew across the country—flew *all night*—to see you. Tell her everything. Don't be stupid or stubborn."

Ben searched his brother's face, the thought of telling Rae he loved her completely overwhelming. Ben hadn't said those three words to anyone in a very long time, not even his brothers.

"I'll tell her if you ask Bonnie out."

Sam pulled out his phone and started thumbing out a message. "Hey, Bonnie," he said slowly as he fumbled over the miniature keyboard. "Want to go grab something to eat when I get back into town?" He glanced up to Ben and returned to his phone. "This is Sam Buttars, by the way, and I'm in...Wy-o-ming." He met Ben's eye. "What else should I say?"

Ben glared and took his brother's phone, very aware that Rae waited only steps away, her eyes not missing a single thing. Sam had indeed typed the message to a contact labeled Bonnie Sherman.

Ben hit send. "Sounds good." He handed the phone back to his brother. Now all he had to do was uphold his end of the deal and tell Rae everything. If only Ben's throat didn't feel stuffed full of cotton.

"This farmhouse is lovely," Rae said as she stepped off the front porch.

"My dad took good care of it. Sam's been payin' someone to keep it up for us all these years." The grass he'd mown a couple of days ago seemed to spring back after he stepped on it. "You want to go out and meet my parents?"

He almost fell over his own feet. He wasn't sure where the words had come from. Did they sound weird? His parents had been dead for a decade.

Rae slipped her hand into Ben's, and every cell in his soul rejoiced to be touching her again. "I'd like that."

They walked in silence, and Ben didn't know how to start a conversation that ended with "I love you." He'd never felt so far out of his element as he did at that moment.

"What are you doing here, Rae?" he asked, his voice gentle and soft.

She took a deep breath and tilted her face toward the deep blue sky. "I quit my job."

Ben did stumble this time and he came to a complete stop. "You did what?" He couldn't seem to find the lie on her face. He couldn't find much more than two things: apprehension and happiness.

"Oh, wait. I have something to show you." She released his hand and jogged away from him. She opened the passenger-side door of her rental car and came back toward him holding a shoe-box. "These are my show medals." She thrust the box toward him.

He took it without looking away from her. He squinted, trying to find a thread to link everything together. Show medals. Flying across the country. Quitting her job.

"Rae, I'm confused."

She'd broken up with him seven days ago, and he could not find a reason for her to be here, giving him her show medals. He did want to see them, though, so he opened the box and peered inside.

"That one's for dressage," she said, pointing to one of the gold ones. "That one's for jumping. I was a good jumper. My horse's name was Evita, and she was this pitch-dark horse with a big attitude. But she loved me, and I loved her, and we worked together really well."

Ben wasn't sure what was going on, but it was good to have Rae beside him, hear her voice. He took a breath and got a few floral notes of her perfume. He looked at Rae. "Where's Evita now?"

Rae's face blanched, and Ben cursed himself for asking the wrong question. "What's this one for?" he asked quickly to cover up his mistake.

"Jumping."

"You got a lot for that."

"Evita was an excellent jumper." A smile blipped across Rae's face. "She loved jumping more than anything. She was a real free spirit."

Ben found himself grinning too. "I bet you liked the jumping as well."

"What makes you say that?"

"You're the type of woman who likes to fly."

"Ben." She said his name with reverence, with love. "I've missed you." She took a step toward him. "I've made a terrible mistake." Another step. One more and she'd practically be in his arms. "Can you forgive me?"

Ben dug for his courage and found he didn't have to go very far. He handed the box of medals back to her. "Why did you come out here?"

"I wanted to talk to you and you wouldn't answer your phone."

"You called?" He hadn't looked at his phone in a couple of days. He wasn't even entirely sure where it was.

"Four times. I eventually went out to Steeple Ridge and talked to Logan and Darren." She glanced over her shoulder. "They told me it was the anniversary of your parents' deaths. I got on a plane a few hours later."

"And you quit your job. When did that happen?"

"Yesterday."

"Yesterday was a big day for you."

She focused on him again, and her mouth barely moved when she said, "The biggest."

He nodded his cowboy hat toward the back fence and started walking again. Rae set her box on the ground and took his hand in hers again. "So I quit my job after I realized I was in love with you."

Ben choked and coughed and froze. He searched Rae's golden-brown eyes and found the love there.

She smiled, one of the shyest he'd seen from her. "I had a choice to make. My job or Ben Buttars." She tiptoed her free fingers up his chest. "Ben Buttars won."

He took her free hand in his and gripped both of her hands. The wind threatened to unseat his cowboy hat, but he couldn't expend any energy on anything but Rae right now. "When did you realize you loved me?"

"About eleven o'clock yesterday morning."

"I was at my parents' graves at that time. I told Sam I was in love with you."

Pure hope lit her eyes. "Really?"

"Really."

"So you're not mad at me?"

"Rae." He dipped his forehead toward hers, but his hat bumped into her first. He took it off and held it at his side. "I've never been mad at you."

"Yes, you have. On the Fourth of July."

"You tried," he said.

"I tried," she said. "But that isn't enough. So I quit."

"You really quit your job?"

"Marched right into Zack's office and told him. Well, not really told him, told him, because he wasn't back yet. But I left a note."

A chuckle burst from Ben's mouth. "What did that note look like?"

"I think it had four words. *Zack, I quit. Rae.*" She added a giggle to his laughter.

Ben's heart expanded to double its size with the sound of her voice, the nearness of her body, the sweet fragrance of her skin. "So you kinda like me."

"No." She sobered. "Ben, I'm in love with you."

"I love you too, Rae." He kissed her, pure joy radiating through him as she deepened the kiss.

24

R ae got drunk on just one of Ben's kisses. She wanted to have his arms around her every morning, every evening. She wanted to giggle and curl into his chest after every kiss. He completed her in a way she didn't know she needed to be completed.

"So my mother loved roses," Ben said, easily taking her hand in his and strolling toward a fence in the distance. "Her favorites were these pink lemonade roses. They really do smell like pink lemonade."

Rae glanced to the row of rose bushes along the back of the house. "They're beautiful."

Everything about Coral Canyon, Wyoming was beautiful. She loved the towering mountains in the distance, and the miles and miles of open land. She hadn't been lying when she said the farmhouse was lovely. It was charming too, and it possessed a spirit she could feel.

Her flight across the country had been lonely and fraught with anxiety. She'd armed herself with a couple changes of clothes and a GPS on her phone. She'd been able to get to Coral

Canyon easily enough, and she'd figured if the small town was anything like Island Park, she'd be able to find the local hot spot and ask about the Buttars' farm.

Sure enough, Gas Station George had been extremely helpful. Still, she'd almost turned around twice, and she'd sat in her rental car for a good five minutes before she'd been able to get herself up to the door.

Now, with Ben's hand in hers and the taste of his mouth on her lips, those discomforts seemed like a distant dot on the horizon.

"This is my mom and dad," he said.

Rae focused on the grave markers in front of her. His father's had been done in a dark gray stone, and his mother's in deep rose. She crouched and ran her fingers along the name of his mother.

"Iris." She glanced up to Ben. "Ironic."

He smiled and knelt on the grass next to her. "This yard was her passion. She was constantly working in vegetable and flower gardens."

"What about your dad?" Rae sat and rolled several blades of grass between her fingers. "Ray Buttars."

"Dad loved the land. Horses and dogs. Fried eggs on toast." Ben chuckled and reached for her hand. "I'm really glad you're here."

"Me too."

"Did you really quit your job?"

She laughed at the way he kept asking and gave his shoulder a gentle shove. "Yes, I did."

"What are you going to do?"

She let the breeze whisper through the tall grass on the other side of the fence. "I don't know. Maybe I can...I don't know. Work on the crew at the Sports Complex."

Ben squeezed her hand. "I can just see you on the riding lawn mower, or driving the tractor with that field rake behind it."

"I've done both of those things."

"I'm sure you have."

"The crew gets off work at three-thirty."

Ben didn't respond right away, and Rae looked at him. "I didn't mean you needed to quit your job," he said so quietly she barely heard him.

"But I did need to quit my job. I just didn't know it until yesterday."

"I don't want you to regret the decision. Start to, I don't know, resent *me* because you quit your job. A job you really like." The worry in his eyes was sweet.

Rae tried to reassure him with her best smile. "It's fine."

"Rae."

"What?"

"What are you going to do, really?"

She shrugged and sighed. "Zack will probably move Burke into my job. If he does that, I can lead the crew at the Sports Complex the way Burke does. Or maybe April. She works nine to five, nothing more. Maybe we could switch places." She glanced up at him. "Or maybe I'll figure out how to sell things online. Or make doughnuts at the shop downtown. It doesn't matter."

"All right," he said, but he sounded more dubious than anything else.

Rae leaned toward him and planted a kiss on his cheek. "Ben, quitting was the right thing to do, I'm sure of it."

"How are you sure?"

"It felt right." She snuggled into his side. "I've been trying to pay more attention to how I feel instead of trying to drive the horse somewhere it shouldn't go."

"Me too," he said. "I think I've been holding on too tight to some things. I'm trying to let them go. You were one of them."

"I don't want you to let me go," she whispered.

"Okay," Ben said in his cowboy drawl, stroking his fingers

from her elbow to her wrist and sending shivers across her skin. "Want to go to the movies with me this afternoon?"

"A movie sounds amazing."

FIVE MONTHS LATER

Rae arrived at the rec center at nine o'clock, the same time she did every morning. She stomped snow and slush from her boots and slicked her hair out of her face. She didn't miss her office, or the stress of organizing youth programs and overseeing the Sports Complex. She still got to see her friends.

She moved around the front desk and went down the hall, lifting her phone from her purse when it chimed. Ben had texted about their upcoming New Year's Eve Sunday dinner at the farm, and whether she'd be able to bring her now-famous chocolate chunk cookies.

Since she'd started her new job at the rec center, she had time and energy to cook. Well, she baked mostly, but Ben didn't complain when he had to eat a peanut butter sandwich on freshly baked bread for dinner.

Sure, no problem, she texted just as April arrived. "Morning, Rae."

She set her purse on her desk and shrugged out of her coat. "Morning. I've got the volleyball flyers ready, and I'll get the info up on the website this morning."

"Great."

Rae sat down to work, where she'd stay for only half the day today, since the rec center was closing at one o'clock so people could spend the Christmas holidays with their families. Rae shared an open space with five desks and four other secretaries. April was the liaison between the work they did in what Rae had lovingly called "the pit" and the administrators down the hall where she used to work.

Zack hadn't moved Burke over, nor had he promoted April. Instead, he'd hired someone new, and Rae really liked Petra, who often came to her with questions.

Later, Ben met her in the parking lot with a bouquet of red roses. "Merry Christmas," he said, leaning down to kiss her.

She cut the kiss short and took the flowers, inhaling their fragrance deep into her soul. "You're okay for dinner tonight with my mom?"

"Yep."

Rae unlocked her car. "Perfect. She's really excited." She started to get in, but Ben reached for her keys. She relinquished them to him, pausing when she saw the frozen look on his face. "You okay?" She put her hand on his forearm.

He jolted as if she'd shocked him with her touch. "Yeah, fine." He hooked her pinky in his and walked her around to the other side of the car.

She tried to engage him in conversation on the way to her house, but he sat rigidly with both hands on the steering wheel and gave short, clipped answers. Rae had learned to read Ben over the past eight months of dating, and she gave up after a couple of attempts at talking. He had something on his mind that he'd unload when he was ready.

"Do you want coffee?" she asked when they finished greeting the pet patrol at the front door. She bypassed the showpiece of her living room—a memory box displaying her show medals.

Ben had made it for her birthday a couple of months ago, revealing another of his hidden talents: woodworking.

"Sure. Coffee sounds great." He followed her into the kitchen while she stepped to the sink to fill the coffee pot.

When she turned, she found him mere inches behind her. "Oh, hey." She nearly slopped water down his chest as she smiled up at him.

"Rae." He took the coffee pot and set it on the counter. "I want to talk to you about something." He put both hands on the counter on either side of her hips, the exact same way he had the first time he'd kissed her.

Her heart catapulted to the back of her tongue, though she'd kissed Ben lots of times. "Okay," she managed to push through her narrow throat.

"It's about what I want for Christmas."

Surprise lifted her eyebrows. "It's Christmas Eve. You're just now telling me?" She'd been asking for weeks what she could get him. Every time, he'd said, "Surprise me."

Well, she'd tried, but she wasn't looking forward to giving him the certificate for a custom saddle fitting at a leather-maker in Burlington. It felt like a lame gift, though he'd probably like it.

He reached up and smoothed her hair behind her ear. "My parents always let us open one gift on Christmas Eve, and we got to choose which one from under this huge tree my mom set up the day after Thanksgiving." He chuckled. "She did things like clockwork, my mom." He cleared his throat. "But I want to give you my gift."

"I don't get to choose?"

"There's only one present." He pressed closer to her, reaching for the cupboard to his right. He stretched up to the top shelf, where she kept old bowls she really should throw out. His eyes shone like the ocean as he pulled his arm back to reveal a small, black ring box.

Rae's breath evaporated, leaving her lungs tight and her throat on fire. When had he put that there? The sneaky devil!

"I love you," he said, his voice teeming with emotion. Her chest quaked in time with the slight tremors in his voice. "I kissed you for the first time right here. I want to shuffle into this kitchen early in the morning and make you coffee while you sleep. I want you to bathe our babies in this sink." He swallowed and glanced at the box, flipping it open to reveal a stunning ring.

"I bought this a few weeks ago, when Sam and I went to Coral Canyon to check on the house. The silver's from the mine above the town, and that's a chocolate diamond. The jeweler didn't say if it was milk or dark, but since milk is clearly superior, we'll go with that." He grinned at her, his voice steady now.

Tears welled in her eyes, and thankfully, she started breathing again.

"I love you," he said again. "All I want for Christmas is for you to say yes." He dropped to one knee, right there in her kitchen. On the floor she hadn't mopped in months.

"Reagan Cantwell, will you marry me?" He watched her with such hope, such love, that Rae's heart swelled and sang.

"Of course," she whispered.

"That's not a yes," he teased.

She laughed and bent down to kiss him. She held his face in her hands and said, "Yes," against his lips. "Yes, yes, yes!"

BOOKS IN THE GOLD VALLEY ROMANCE SERIES:

Before the Leap: A Gold Valley Romance (Book 1): Jace Lovell only has one thing left after his fiancé abandons him at the altar: his job at Horseshoe Home Ranch. He throws himself into becoming the best foreman the ranch has ever had—and that includes hiring an interior designer to make the ranch owner's wife happy. Belle Edmunds is back in Gold Valley and she's desperate to build a portfolio that she can use to start her own firm in Montana. She applies for the job at Horseshoe Home, and though Jace and Belle grew up together, they've never seen eye to eye on much more than the sky is blue. Jace isn't anywhere near forgiving his fiancé, and he's not sure he's ready for a new relationship with someone as fiery and beautiful as Belle. Can she employ her patience while he figures out how to forgive so they can find their own brand of happily-ever-after?

After the Fall: A Gold Valley Romance (Book 2): Professional snowboarder Sterling Maughan has sequestered himself in his family's cabin in the exclusive mountain community above Gold Valley, Montana after a devastating fall that ended his career. Lost, with no direction and no motivation, the last thing he wants is company. But Norah Watson has other plans for the cabin. Not only does she clean Sterling's cabin, she's a counselor at Silver Creek, a teen rehabilitation center at the base of the mountain that uses horses to aid in the rebuilding of lives, and she brings her girls up to the cabin every twelve weeks. When Sterling finds out there's a job for an at-risk counselor at Silver Creek, he asks Norah to drive him back and forth. He learns to ride horses and use equine therapy to help his boys—and himself. The more time they spend together, the more convinced Norah is to never tell Sterling about her troubled past, let him see her house on the wrong side of the tracks, or meet her mother. But Sterling is interested in all things Norah, and as his body heals, so does his faith. Will Norah be able to trust Sterling so they can have a chance at true love?

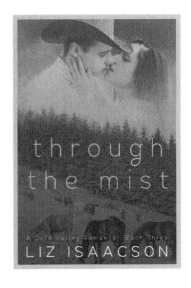

Through the Mist: A Gold Valley Romance (Book 3): Landon Edmunds has been a cowboy his whole life. An accident five years ago ended his successful rodeo career, and now he's looking to start a horse ranch of his own, and he's looking outside of Montana. Which would be great if God hadn't brought Megan Palmer back to Gold Valley right when Landon is looking to leave. As the preacher's daughter, Megan isn't that excited to be back in her childhood hometown. Megan and Landon work together well, and as sparks fly, she's sure God brought her back to Gold Valley so she could find her happily ever after. Through serious discussion and prayer, can Landon and Megan find their future together?

Be sure to check out the spinoff series, the Brush Creek Brides romances after you read THROUGH THE MIST. Start with A WEDDING FOR THE WIDOWER.

Between the Reins: A Gold Valley Romance (Book 4): Twelve years ago, Owen Carr left Gold Valley—and his long-time girlfriend—in favor of a country music career in Nashville. Married and divorced, Natalie teaches ballet at the dance studio in Gold Valley, but she never auditioned for the professional company the way she dreamed of doing. With Owen back, she realizes all the opportunities she missed out on when he left all those years ago —including a future with him. Can they mend broken bridges in order to have a second chance at love?

Over the Moon: A Gold Valley Romance (Book 5): Holly Gray is back in Gold Valley after her failed engagement five years ago. She just needs her internship hours on the ranch so she can finish her veterinarian degree and return to Vermont. She wasn't planning on rekindling many friendships, and she certainly wasn't planning on running into a familiar face at Horseshoe Home Ranch. But it's not the face she was dreading seeing—it's his twin brother, Caleb Chamberlain. Caleb knows Holly was his twin's fiancé at one point, but he can't deny the sparks between them. Can they navigate a rocky and secret past to find a future together?

Journey to Steeple Ridge Farm with Holly — and fall in love with the cowboys there in the Steeple Ridge Romance series! Start with STARTING OVER AT STEEPLE RIDGE.

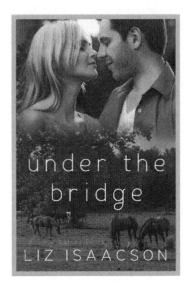

Under the Bridge: A Gold Valley Romance (Book 6): Ty Barker has been dancing through the last thirty years of his life--and he's suddenly realized he's alone. River Lee Whitely is back in Gold Valley with her two little girls after a divorce that's left deep scars. She has a job at Silver Creek that requires her to be able to ride a horse, and she nearly tramples Ty at her first lesson. That's just fine by him, because River Lee is the girl Ty has never gotten over. Ty realizes River Lee needs time to settle into her new job, her new home, her new life as a single parent, but going slow has never been his style. But for River Lee, can Ty take the necessary steps to keep her in his life?

Up on the Housetop: A Gold Valley Romance (Book 7): Archer Bailey has already lost one job to Emersyn Enders, so he deliberately doesn't tell her about the cowhand job up at Horseshoe Home Ranch. Emery's temporary job is ending, but her obligations to her physically disabled sister aren't. As Archer and Emery work together, its clear that the sparks flying between them aren't all from their friendly competition over a job. Will Emery and Archer be able to navigate the ranch, their close quarters, and their individual circumstances to find love this holiday season?

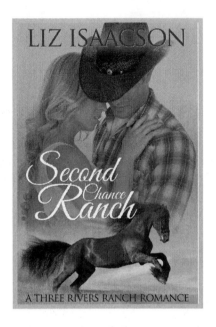

**Second Chance Ranch: A Three Rivers Ranch Romance (Book
1):** After his deployment, injured and discharged Major Squire
Ackerman returns to Three Rivers Ranch, wanting to forgive
Kelly for ignoring him a decade ago. He'd like to provide the
stable life she needs, but with old wounds opening and a ranch
on the brink of financial collapse, it will take patience and faith to
make their second chance possible.

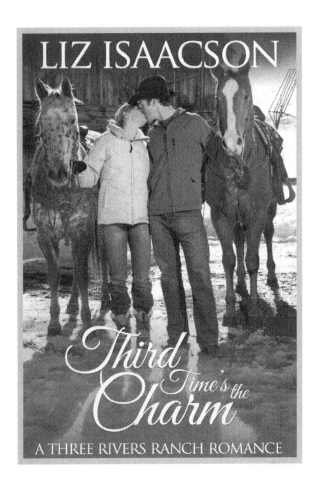

Third Time's the Charm: A Three Rivers Ranch Romance (Book 2): First Lieutenant Peter Marshall has a truckload of debt and no way to provide for a family, but Chelsea helps him see past all the obstacles, all the scars. With so many unknowns, can Pete and Chelsea develop the love, acceptance, and faith needed to find their happily ever after?

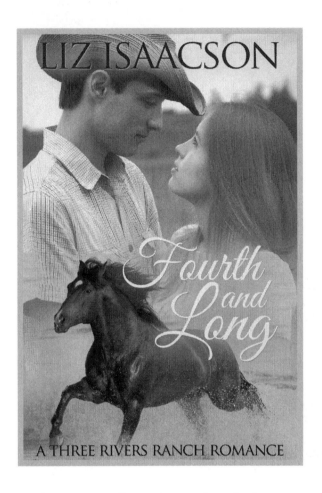

Fourth and Long: A Three Rivers Ranch Romance (Book 3): Commander Brett Murphy goes to Three Rivers Ranch to find some rest and relaxation with his Army buddies. Having his ex-wife show up with a seven-year-old she claims is his son is anything but the R&R he craves. Kate needs to make amends, and Brett needs to find forgiveness, but are they too late to find their happily ever after?

Fifth Generation Cowboy: A Three Rivers Ranch Romance (Book 4): Tom Lovell has watched his friends find their true happiness on Three Rivers Ranch, but everywhere he looks, he only sees friends. Rose Reyes has been bringing her daughter out to the ranch for equine therapy for months, but it doesn't seem to be working. Her challenges with Mari are just as frustrating as ever. Could Tom be exactly what Rose needs? Can he remove his friendship blinders and find love with someone who's been right in front of him all this time?

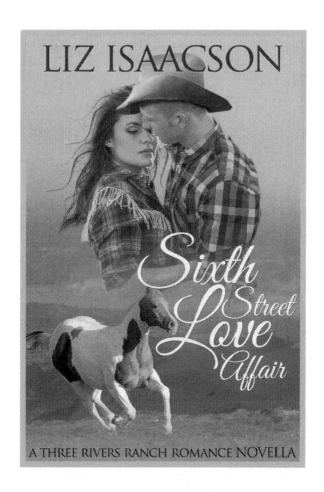

LIZ ISAACSON

Sixth Street Love Affair

A THREE RIVERS RANCH ROMANCE NOVELLA

Sixth Street Love Affair: A Three Rivers Ranch Romance (Book 5): After losing his wife a few years back, Garth Ahlstrom thinks he's ready for a second chance at love. But Juliette Thompson has a secret that could destroy their budding relationship. Can they find the strength, patience, and faith to make things work?

The Seventh Sergeant: A Three Rivers Ranch Romance (Book 6): Life has finally started to settle down for Sergeant Reese Sanders after his devastating injury overseas. Discharged from the Army and now with a good job at Courage Reins, he's finally found happiness—until a horrific fall puts him right back where he was years ago: Injured and depressed. Carly Watters, Reese's new veteran care coordinator, dislikes small towns almost as much as she loathes cowboys. But she finds herself faced with both when she gets assigned to Reese's case. Do they have the humility and faith to make their relationship more than professional?

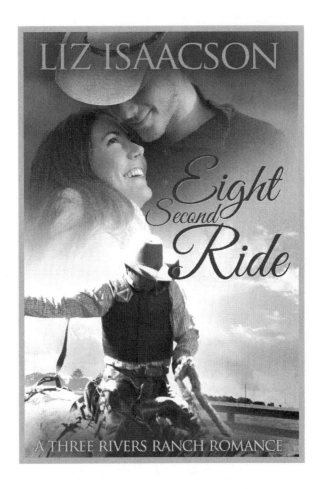

Eight Second Ride: A Three Rivers Ranch Romance (Book 7): Ethan Greene loves his work at Three Rivers Ranch, but he can't seem to find the right woman to settle down with. When sassy yet vulnerable Brynn Bowman shows up at the ranch to recruit him back to the rodeo circuit, he takes a different approach with the barrel racing champion. His patience and newfound faith pay off when a friendship--and more--starts with Brynn. But she wants out of the rodeo circuit right when Ethan wants to rejoin. Can they find the path God wants them to take and still stay together?

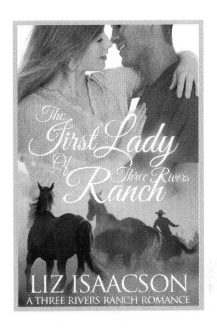

The First Lady of Three Rivers Ranch: A Three Rivers Ranch Romance (Book 8): Heidi Duffin has been dreaming about opening her own bakery since she was thirteen years old. She scrimped and saved for years to afford baking and pastry school in San Francisco. And now she only has one year left before she's a certified pastry chef. Frank Ackerman's father has recently retired, and he's taken over the largest cattle ranch in the Texas Panhandle. A horseman through and through, he's also nearing thirty-one and looking for someone to bring love and joy to a homestead that's been dominated by men for a decade. But when he convinces Heidi to come clean the cowboy cabins, she changes all that. But the siren's call of a bakery is still loud in Heidi's ears, even if she's also seeing a future with Frank. Can she rely on her faith in ways she's never had to before or will their relationship end when summer does?

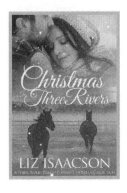

Christmas in Three Rivers: A Three Rivers Ranch Romance (Book 9): Isn't Christmas the best time to fall in love? The cowboys of Three Rivers Ranch think so. Join four of them as they journey toward their path to happily ever after in four, all-new novellas in the Amazon #1 Bestselling Three Rivers Ranch Romance series.

THE NINTH INNING: The Christmas season has never felt like such a burden to boutique owner Andrea Larsen. But with Mama gone and the holidays upon her, Andy finds herself wishing she hadn't been so quick to judge her former boyfriend, cowboy Lawrence Collins. Well, Lawrence hasn't forgotten about Andy either, and he devises a plan to get her out to the ranch so they can reconnect. Do they have the faith and humility to patch things up and start a new relationship?

TEN DAYS IN TOWN: Sandy Keller is tired of the dating scene in Three Rivers. Though she owns the pancake house, she's looking for a fresh start, which means an escape from the town where she grew up. When her older brother's best friend, Tad Jorgensen, comes to town for the holidays, it is a balm to his weary soul. A helicopter tour guide who experienced a near-death experience, he's looking to start over too--but in Three Rivers. Can Sandy and Tad navigate their troubles to find the path God wants them to take--and discover true love--in only ten days?

ELEVEN YEAR REUNION: Pastry chef extraordinaire, Grace

Lewis has moved to Three Rivers to help Heidi Ackerman open a bakery in Three Rivers. Grace relishes the idea of starting over in a town where no one knows about her failed cupcakery. She doesn't expect to run into her old high school boyfriend, Jonathan Carver. A carpenter working at Three Rivers Ranch, Jon's in town against his will. But with Grace now on the scene, Jon's thinking life in Three Rivers is suddenly looking up. But with her focus on baking and his disdain for small towns, can they make their eleven year reunion stick?

THE TWELFTH TOWN: Newscaster Taryn Tucker has had enough of life on-screen. She's bounced from town to town before arriving in Three Rivers, completely alone and completely anonymous--just the way she now likes it. She takes a job cleaning at Three Rivers Ranch, hoping for a chance to figure out who she is and where God wants her. When she meets happy-go-lucky cowhand Kenny Stockton, she doesn't expect sparks to fly. Kenny's always been "the best friend" for his female friends, but the pull between him and Taryn can't be denied. Will they have the courage and faith necessary to make their opposite worlds mesh?

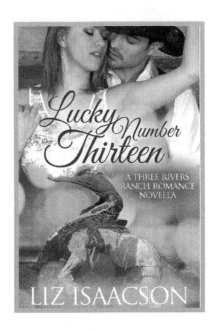

Lucky Number Thirteen: A Three Rivers Ranch Romance (Book 10): Tanner Wolf, a rodeo champion ten times over, is excited to be riding in Three Rivers for the first time since he left his philandering ways and found religion. Seeing his old friends Ethan and Brynn is therapuetic--until a terrible accident lands him in the hospital. With his rodeo career over, Tanner thinks maybe he'll stay in town--and it's not just because his nurse, Summer Hamblin, is the prettiest woman he's ever met. But Summer's the queen of first dates, and as she looks for a way to make a relationship with the transient rodeo star work Summer's not sure she has the fortitude to go on a second date. Can they find love among the tragedy?

BOOKS IN THE BRUSH CREEK BRIDES ROMANCE SERIES:

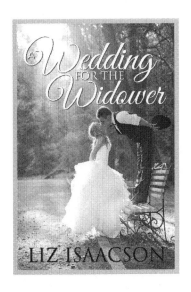

A Wedding for the Widower: Brush Creek Brides Romance (Book 1): Former rodeo champion and cowboy Walker Thompson trains horses at Brush Creek Horse Ranch, where he lives a simple life in his cabin with his ten-year-old son. A widower of six years, he's worked with Tess Wagner, a widow who came to Brush Creek to escape the turmoil of her life to give her seven-year-old son a slower pace of life. But Tess's breast cancer is back...

Walker will have to decide if he'd rather spend even a short time with Tess than not have her in his life at all. Tess wants to feel God's love and power, but can she discover and accept God's will in order to find her happy ending?

A Companion for the Cowboy: Brush Creek Brides Romance (Book 2): Cowboy and professional roper Justin Jackman has found solitude at Brush Creek Horse Ranch, preferring his time with the animals he trains over dating. With two failed engagements in his past, he's not really interested in getting his heart stomped on again. But when flirty and fun Renee Martin picks him up at a church ice cream bar--on a bet, no less-- he finds himself more than just

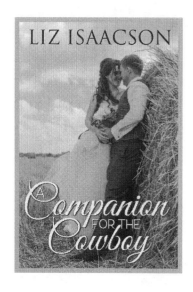

a little interested. His Gen-X attitudes are attractive to her; her Millennial behaviors drive him nuts. Can Justin look past their differences and take a chance on another engagement?

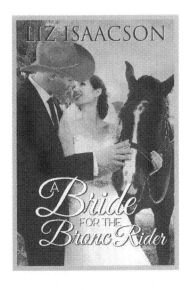

A Bride for the Bronc Rider: Brush Creek Brides Romance (Book 3): Ted Caldwell has been a retired bronc rider for years, and he thought he was perfectly happy training horses to buck at Brush Creek Ranch. He was wrong. When he meets April Nox, who comes to the ranch to hide her pregnancy from all her friends back in Jackson Hole, Ted realizes he has a huge family-shaped hole in his life. April is embarrassed, heartbroken, and trying to find her extinguished faith. She's never ridden a horse and wants nothing to do with a cowboy ever again. Can Ted and April create a family of happiness and love from a tragedy?

A Family for the Farmer: Brush Creek Brides Romance (Book 4): Blake Gibbons oversees all the agriculture at Brush Creek Horse Ranch, sometimes moonlighting as a general contractor. When he meets Erin Shields, new in town, at her aunt's bakery, he's instantly smitten. Erin moved to Brush Creek after a divorce that left her penniless, homeless, and a single mother of three children under age eight. She's nowhere near ready to start dating again, but the 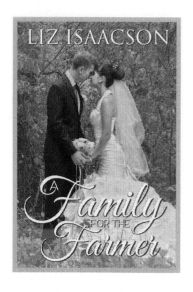 longer Blake hangs around the bakery, the more she starts to like him. Can Blake and Erin find a way to blend their lifestyles and become a family?

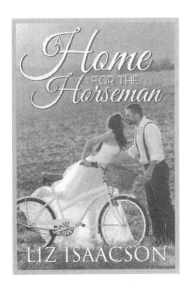

A Home for the Horseman: Brush Creek Brides Romance (Book 5): Emmett Graves has always had a positive outlook on life. He adores training horses to become barrel racing champions during the day and cuddling with his cat at night. Fresh off her professional rodeo retirement, Molly Brady comes to Brush Creek Horse Ranch as Emmett's protege. He's not thrilled, and she's allergic to cats. Oh, and she'd like to stay cowboy-free, thank you very much. But Emmett's about as cowboy as they come.... Can Emmett and Molly work together without falling in love?

A Refuge for the Rancher: Brush Creek Brides Romance (Book 6): Grant Ford spends his days training cattle—when he's not camped out at the elementary school hoping to catch a glimpse of his ex-girlfriend. When principal Shannon Sharpe confronts him and asks him to stay away from the school, the spark between them is instant and hot. Shannon's expecting a transfer very soon, but she also needs a summer outdoor coordinator—and

Grant fits the bill. Just because he's handsome and everything Shannon's ever wanted in a cowboy husband means nothing. Will Grant and Shannon be able to survive the summer or will the Utah heat be too much for them to handle?

ABOUT LIZ

Liz Isaacson writes inspirational romance, usually set in Texas, or Montana, or anywhere else horses and cowboys exist. She lives in Utah, where she teaches elementary school, taxis her daughter to dance several times a week, and eats a lot of Ferrero Rocher while writing. Find her on her website at lizisaacson.com.

67907995R00139

Made in the USA
Middletown, DE
26 March 2018